ALSO BY

DOMENICO STARNONE

Trick
Ties

TRUST

Domenico Starnone

TRUST

Translated from the Italian
by Jhumpa Lahiri

Europa
editions

Europa Editions
1 Penn Plaza, Suite 6282
New York, N.Y. 10019
www.europaeditions.com
info@europaeditions.com

Copyright © 2019 by Giulio Einaudi editore s.p.a., Torino
First Publication 2021 by Europa Editions

Translation by Jhumpa Lahiri
Original title: *Confidenza*
Translation copyright © 2021 by Europa Editions

Library of Congress Cataloging in Publication Data is available
ISBN 978-1-60945-703-7

Starnone, Domenico
· Trust

Book design by Emanuele Ragnisco
www.mekkanografici.com

Cover illustration © nerosunero (Mario Sughi)

Prepress by Grafica Punto Print – Rome

Printed in Italy

CONTENTS

TRUST

THE FIRST STORY

1.

Love, well, what to say? We talk about it a lot, but I don't think I've used the word much, on the contrary, I doubt it's ever been of any use to me, though I've loved, of course, I've loved, I've loved until I've lost my mind and my wits. Love as I've known it, in fact, is a lava of crude life that burns the refined one, an eruption that obliterates understanding and piety, reason and rights, geography and history, sickness and health, richer and poorer, exceptions and rules. All that's left is a yearning that twists and distorts, an obsession without a cure: where is she, where isn't she, what's she thinking, doing, what did she say, what did she really mean when she said that, what isn't she telling me, was she as happy to see me as I was to see her, and feeling better now that I've left, or has my absence debilitated her instead, as hers debilitates me, annihilating me, stripping me of all the energy that her presence, on the other hand, generates, and what am I without her, a stopped clock on the corner of a busy street, oh her voice on the other hand, oh to stand next to her, to diminish the distance between us, reduce it to nothing, erase kilometers, meters, centimeters, millimeters, and melt, lose myself, stop being myself, in fact, it already feels like I was never myself other than within her, in the pleasure of her, and this makes me proud, it cheers me up, and it depresses me, it saddens me, and then it jolts me again, it electrifies me, I care so much for her, yes, all I want is the best for her, always, whatever happens, even if she turns cold, even if she loves other people, even if she humiliates me, even if she strips me of everything, even of the very capacity to care for her. Absurd, the things that can take place in your head: to want the best for someone even when you don't want them anymore, to want the worst even when you care. It's happened to me, which is why I've dodged the word as often as possible. I don't know what to do with seraphic love, comforting love, love that rings out from the rooftops, love that purifies, pathetic love: extraneousness has kept me from using the word much in my long life. On the other hand, I've used several others—yearning, fury, languor, bewilderment, necessity, urgency, desire—too many, I fear, I'm fishing through five thousand years of writing, and god knows I could keep going. But now I'm forced to move on to Teresa, she's the one who always refused to stay put inside that combination of four letters, and yet she lays claim to it, she still lays claims to it, a thousand times over.

I'd already fallen for Teresa when she sat at a desk next to the window and proved to be one of my liveliest students. But I only realized it when, a year after graduating, she called me, came to wait for me at the school, told me about her turbulent times at university as we were walking on a fine autumn day, and suddenly kissed me. It was that kiss that formally began our relationship, which lasted, all in all, for about three years, caught between needs never truly satisfied—of reciprocal, absolute possession—and tensions that would end up in fights, bites, and tears. I remember one evening in the home of acquaintants, we were a group of seven or eight, and I was sitting next to a girl, originally from Arles, who'd been in Rome for a few months and had such an incredibly seductive way of mangling her Italian that all I'd wanted to do was listen to her voice. Instead, everyone was talking, Teresa most of all, saying, in her usual expansive way, very intelligent things with extreme precision. I must admit that for some months that desire of hers, to always be at the center, ratcheting up the level of even the most frivolous conversations, had begun to irk me, which was why I tended to interrupt her often, with some joking remark, but she glowered at me and said, excuse me, I'm talking. On that occasion, maybe I interrupted her one too many times, since I liked the girl from Arles and wanted her to like me. Then Teresa turned to me, furious, seizing the bread knife and shouting: try to cut off what I'm saying one more time and I'll cut out your tongue and then some. We faced off in public as if we were alone, and today I believe we really were, such was the extent that we were absorbed with each other, for good and for ill. Our acquaintances were there, sure, and the girl from Arles, but they were inessential figures, all that mattered was our ongoing attraction and repulsion. It was as if our boundless admiration for each other only served to ascertain that we loathed each other, and vice versa.

Naturally there were plenty of happy times, and we talked about everything, we kidded around, I tickled her until she gave me long kisses to make me stop. But it didn't last, we ourselves were the agitators of our life together. We seemed convinced that the intensity with which we continuously rocked the boat would have transformed us, in the end, into the ideal couple, but we never got closer to that goal, it just slipped increasingly out of reach. The time that I discovered, thanks to some gossip from the very girl from Arles, that Teresa had been seen behaving in an excessively intimate way with a well-known skinny hunchbacked academic, with crooked teeth, weak eyes, and spidery fingers with which he played the piano for his adoring female students, I was overcome with such repugnance for her that I came home and without explanation grabbed her by the hair, dragged her to the bathroom, wanted to scrub her down myself, every millimeter of her body, with detergent from Marseilles. I didn't yell at her, I spoke with my usual irony, saying: I can look the other way, do whatever you want, but not with someone so disgusting. And she wrested herself free, she kicked, she slapped and scratched me, yelling, so this is who you really are, shame on you, shame on you.

We fought, that time, in a way that seemed to end it, you couldn't go back after what we'd slung at each other. And yet, even that time, we patched it up. We clung to each other until dawn, laughing at the girl from Arles, at the pianist and cytology teacher. But now we were scared; we'd risked losing each other. And I think it was that fear that prompted us, right after that, to find a way to nail down our codependence for good.

Teresa cautiously put forward a plan. She said: let's say I tell you a secret, something so awful that I've never even told it to myself, but then you have to confide something just as horrible to me, something that would destroy your life if anyone came to know it. She smiled, as if she were inviting me to play a game, but deep down she was quite tense. Her anxiety was contagious, I was stunned, I was concerned that, at only twenty-three years of age, she could already have a secret so very unmentionable. I, at thirty, had one, and it had to do with an affair so embarrassing that I blushed just thinking about it. I stared down at the tips of my shoes and waited for that disturbing feeling to pass. We beat around the bush for a bit, asking who would be the first to confide to the other.

—You go first, she said, in that imperiously ironic way that she had when she was bursting with affection.

—No, you first, I have to determine if your secret is as awful as mine.

—And why do I have to trust you and not the other way around?

—Because I know my secret and I don't believe you have one as horrible.

In the end, a back and forth, and then she caved, irritated, above all—I wager—that I didn't believe she was capable of such an unspeakable deed. I let her talk, never interrupting, and when she was done, I couldn't come up with a single word worthy of a response.

—So?

—It's awful.

—I told you. Now it's your turn. And if you tell me something silly, I'm leaving and you'll never see me again.

I confided in her, first in fragments, then in greater detail, I didn't want to stop talking, she was the one who told me to stop. I sighed heavily and said:

—Now you know something about me that no one else does.

—The same goes for you.

—We can never split up now, we're really beholden to each other.

—Yes.

—Aren't you happy?

—Yes.

—It was your idea.

—Of course.

—I love you.

—Me too.

—So much.

—So so much.

A few days later, without arguing, on the contrary, using courteous language that we'd never used before, we told each other that our relationship had reached its end, and we agreed, mutually, to break up.

2.

At first I was relieved. Teresa, all told, was a disobedient and quarrelsome girl who balked at everything I said, who quipped sarcastically at all my shortcomings. Not to mention the fact that she squabbled not only with me but with everyone: shopkeepers, postal workers, traffic cops, the police, neighbors, friends that mattered to me. She intensified these conflicts with a little laugh that seemed cheerful but seethed with anger instead, a guttural noise, like a caesura, that punctuated sentences thick with insults. At least a couple times I came to blows with riffraff who forgot that they were dealing with a girl. But then days and weeks passed and the relief dwindled and I'd start to miss her. Or rather, I felt that the space demarcated by her in her one-room apartment where we'd lived, or the space beside me on the street, at the movies, everywhere I turned, was empty and grey. What a mess, a friend once said to me, falling in love with a girl who, in all respects, is more alive than we are. My friend was right: even though I wasn't exactly lackluster, Teresa contained a surplus of vital energy, and when she overflowed nothing could hold her back. This was a beautiful thing, and I missed it, once in a while I longed to see her again. But just as I was starting to convince myself that there was no harm in calling her, I crossed paths with Nadia.

Regarding Nadia, I don't want to get into it much: she was shy, she played it close to the vest, even in the way she said good morning, and she was extremely kind, the opposite of Teresa. I met her at school, she'd graduated with a degree in mathematics and it was her first job. At first, I didn't notice her, she was a far cry from the women I'm typically attracted to, and she didn't really belong to those politically, artistically, and sexually audacious times that had swept me up, before, during, and after my relationship with Teresa. Nevertheless, something about her—hard to say what, maybe the flush in her cheeks she could never conceal—appealed to me, slightly more each week, and I started to gravitate toward her. I probably thought I could shield her from that tendency to blush by teaching her to transgress in all areas of her life, in words and even in deeds. I'd never taught Teresa anything, even though I was seven years older, even though she'd been my student in the same high school where I still taught. And this had disheartened me at times, she seemed to know it all, whereas Nadia was enclosed in a circle whose diameter was quite small, beyond which she'd never ventured.

I started off with polite sentences, then I cracked a few jokes, and that led to my asking her out for coffee during one of our breaks. One coffee followed another, it became a routine, and I realized it meant more to her than to me. And so, one day I waited a few hours for her to finish working, and I asked if she wanted to have lunch at a trattoria close to the school. She said no, she was busy, and I discovered, on that occasion, that she had a boyfriend whom she planned to marry the following autumn. I told her the story, on my end, of how I'd deeply loved a woman with whom I'd hoped to spend my life, but that things hadn't gone the right way, it was all over, and yet I was still torn up about it. Given that she was rather intrigued by my suffering, I let another week pass, I invited her again, and this time she said yes. I remember that at lunch she was nervously cheerful and laughed at everything I said. While we waited for the second course, I put my hand on the table, a few millimeters away from hers.

—Can I kiss your palm? I asked, grazing her pinky with mine on the white tablecloth next to a glass filled with wine.

—Why, what are you saying!—she exclaimed, withdrawing her hand so suddenly that the wineglass would have tipped over had I not grabbed onto it with a quick reflex that surprised me. I replied:

—Because I feel like it.

—You should have kept it to yourself, it's foolish, you can't tell people everything you want.

—Some foolish things are lovely both to say and do.

—Foolish things are and always will be foolish.

A categorical sentence, but uttered with sweetness: she was

kind even when she scolded people. After lunch she wanted to go home on the bus, but I offered her a ride in my beat-up Renault 4. She agreed, and as soon as we were sitting inside next to each other I went about trying to take her hand again, more determined. This time she didn't withdraw it, maybe because she was stunned more than anything, and I gave a delicate turn to her wrist, I draw her palm to my lips, but instead of kissing it, I licked it. Then I looked at her, waiting for her to protest, disgusted, and instead I detected a faint smile on her face.

—I was just playing around, I said in my defense, suddenly uneasy.

—Of course.

—Did you like it?

—Yes.

—But you think it's foolish.

—Yes.

—Well then?

—Do it again.

I licked her palm again, then I tried to kiss her, but she pushed me away. She murmured that she couldn't, she felt guilty about her boyfriend, they'd been happily together for six years. Then she went on to tell me a great deal about him: he'd been a promising basketball player, then he decided he liked studying more than sports and now he was a young chemist who worked for an important manufacturer and earned an excellent living. That last detail upset me, it was as if she wanted to point out that I, in contrast, was only a high-school literature teacher and didn't have the right to chat her up and drag her down a wayward path. I kept trying to kiss her, and since she kept turning her face away, I cried out:

—It's only a kiss, what's the big deal?

—A kiss is a kiss.

—I'll just touch the tip of my tongue to your front teeth.

—No.

—Then how about if I barely, just barely touch your lip.

—Leave me alone.

—What's wrong with an affectionate exchange?

—It would hurt Carlo, that's what's wrong.

Carlo was the brilliant chemist she'd loved for years. She said she'd always been faithful to him and had no intention of ruining a solid relationship for my sake. I protested:

—A kiss is enough to hurt him? Does he think he owns your mouth, your tongue?

—It's not a question of ownership, but of humiliation. If you had a girlfriend, wouldn't she feel humiliated?

—If I had one and she felt humiliated, I'd leave her right away. Where's the humiliation?

She thought about it. She whispered:

—A kiss is shorthand for intercourse.

—So, you're saying if we kiss, we fuck?

—Symbolically, yes.

—I think that's taking it too far. And anyway, symbolic intercourse never hurts anyone. If Carlo is so vulnerable, just don't tell him.

—Are you suggesting that I lie to him?

—Lies are the salvation of humanity.

—I never lie.

—Then you have to tell him that I licked your palm.

—Why?

—Because not the first time but the second, I did it with symbolic intention.

She turned red and stared at me, disoriented, and I took advantage to kiss her lightly on the mouth. Since she didn't pull away, I pressed my lower lip between her lips, I held it there a few seconds, then I let the tip of my tongue slip inside her. I was about to retreat, and take stock of that brief exploration, when Nadia herself stuck her tongue—alive and smooth and warm—into my mouth with determination. And now she was already putting her arms around my neck, her lips clung, pressing firmly, and our tongues played cat and mouse ransacking every nook of our mouths. When she disentangled herself—she did this by throwing back her head, as if to evade a blow—I saw another aspect to her face, her features had relaxed, her eyes were defiant and, at the same time, as if awakened in that moment, trying to escape from a torpor that had won her over. I tried to pull her toward me again, but she resisted. I said, please, one more time, but she didn't want to. I started the car and took her home.

3.

That kiss, a mere ten minutes later, had already provoked such an enormous thirst for her that I myself was amazed. Our connection had seemed nothing but playful, but instead it had turned pressing, and not a day passed that I didn't invite her to lunch, dinner, or the movies. Since she always politely turned me down, one morning I stopped her in her path in an empty hallway, and I said:

—I really like you.

—I like you, too.

—So why do you run away?

—Because you're hurting me.

That hurt, she explained, derived from the fact that she loved Carlo, and the love she felt for me was wearing down her love for him. After that long explanation full of anguished stammering, to which I replied that not only did I really like her but felt now that I loved her, she agreed to have dinner with me at an elegant place I knew.

It was winter, cold and rainy, but when we were almost at the restaurant I pulled into a dark narrow street and turned off the ignition. She told me, softly, to turn the car on again, and I said fine, but I tried to embrace her. She pushed me away, laughed, then whispered that she wanted to rest, only for a minute, peacefully, with her head on my shoulder. We arranged ourselves so that, even though she sat on her seat and I on mine, we could fulfil that desire. But as soon as she was settled, I drew my lips to hers and we had a long kiss. I realized, surprised, that I really did love her, and that I didn't want to ever stop kissing her.

Until a few months before, I thought I'd loved Teresa, who was tall and, albeit thin, large everywhere: the shoulders, the thighs, the breasts; a woman who disdained convention and never minced words, who barely tolerated not only when people wronged her but above all when they wronged others; who considered sex an unbridled expression of merrymaking and not a matter of importance. Now, on the contrary, I thought I loved Nadia, whose body was, instead, small; she was measured, careful not to speak unpleasantly; and as for sex—by now it was clear to me—even letting me take her hand, letting me lace my fingers with hers, struck her as the start of a chain of complex implications that could rearrange your entire existence. It was no use saying to myself: take it easy, think, you can't go from one kind of woman to her exact opposite. The fact that Nadia was such a far cry from Teresa inexplicably moved me. I felt that she was a little girl, a small Nadia perpetually afraid of possible punishment. Consequently, I savored those kisses as I never had before, and in order to prevent her from pulling away and cutting off the contact between our mouths, I avoided all attempts to seek her out with my hands through her thick, protective down coat. She was the one who, at a certain point, breathing onto me through her lips, said, let's eat, and I said, hoarse with emotion: let's go.

We headed toward the trattoria, which was at the top of a narrow street. It was getting colder and colder and I took her

arm as we walked toward the gaudily lit entrance. I said, avoid-
ing irony, as I no longer craved irony:

—I'm all stirred up.

—Are you upset?

—No, I'm happy, but wanting you turns me on my head.
Aren't you stirred up?

—How do you mean?

—Flustered, you know what I mean.

—Can I not answer that?

—Whisper it in my ear.

—I'm not telling you anything.

—Please.

I leaned down, putting my ear next to her mouth. Nadia
stuck her tongue into it, and I pulled away immediately, drying
it out with my finger.

—Happy now?

We went back and shut ourselves up in the car; we never
went to the restaurant. The next day, as soon as we saw each
other at school, she told me she'd told her boyfriend everything, it was impossible for her to lie to him.

—What do you mean by everything?

—Everything.

I asked her to marry me.

4.

A week before the wedding I bumped into Teresa. I'd just
left the school and I was walking toward my car, chatting with
three of my students, when she passed by on her Vespa, on the
other side of the street, and she slowed down, shouting out:
Pietro, you wretch, so you're still alive. And I—maybe
because she was all bundled up—turned around to see if the
woman who'd shouted "Pietro, you wretch, so you're still

alive" was pissed at me or at someone else. She must have seen me do this, because when I said goodbye to my students and crossed the street to join her, she said, in her usual ironic way, pretending to be remorseful: after swearing ten thousand times that you'd love me forever, you took less than a year to forget me. I defended myself, blaming her hood, her scarf, her heavy jacket, and after some generic chitchat I tried to peel away. But Teresa said there was a new rotisserie where the arancini were delicious and with her typical imperiousness announced: hop on, five minutes, we'll have a bite and then I'll take you back to your car.

It was wrong to obey her. It took just a few seconds for our bodies to trust each other again; I recognized the smell of her hair from the wisps that poked out of her hood, and I listened once more to her voice, immediately carried off by the wind, that said: don't hold onto my hips, you idiot, we'll fall over that way. I'd always loved it when she took me for a ride on her Vespa. At the start of our relationship, she was willing to take me everywhere, and it was nice feeling her between my legs. Sometimes when we weren't fighting, I kissed her neck, I rested my head on her back, and she did her part by adjusting herself on the seat so that she was pressed against me as much as possible. In brief, I was moved to see her again. I realized that though our love had ended, the friendship hadn't, at least a friendship that's nourished by a physically intimate past, that sometimes lets you retain, without embarrassment, an everlasting trust. I started to tell her about a brief essay on the state of Italian schools, a minor piece of work I'd produced by the by, if only to keep my mind busy after we'd split up, and I summarized it for her, taking a long while to do so, so that she said, amused, well it doesn't sound so brief or trifling to me! After that I proceeded to tell her about my mother's sudden death, something that had happened two months ago, and this, yes, I recounted in a few matter-of-fact sentences leaving her space to carry on with sincere words of consolation. Finally, I told her that I was about to get married and talked at length about Nadia.

She, too, seemed at ease. She told me she was about to leave for the United States; she'd received a scholarship from a university in Wisconsin. She talked wittily about a boyfriend—he was also a student—of veterinary medicine. He'd told her: it's either me or the United States, and she'd told him with no hesitation, The United States. She appeared happy to hear about my marriage, saying: you were born with a silver spoon, now you've finally found a foolish woman who has no idea how dangerous you are. This last thing she said somewhat troubled me, but I did nothing to betray it, rather, I laughed, agreeing with her, and murmured: I've learned to conceal myself more effectively. But she also realized that she had said something which, in spite of its lighthearted tone, might have sounded unkind, and attempted—and this was something new—to make up for it:

—On the other hand, you have many lovely qualities, and if you let them rise to the surface, this Nadia could be the lucky one.

We bantered back and forth like this for a while longer, and then she took me back to my car. There was traffic, and when she wove through it, when I was afraid that my knees would collide into the sides of a car or a bus, I'd press up against her thighs and feel reassured. At one point I rested my cheek on her back and remembered the evening before my mother's death. For a few seconds I fell asleep.

—I had fun, I told her when we reached my car, saying goodbye.

—Me too.

—Enjoy yourself in America.

—And you try to behave with Nadia. Don't torment her the way you tormented me.

—What are you talking about, I loved you very much.

—You could have been better.

—But also worse.

—No doubt. Which is why, don't forget, if you step out of line with that poor girl, I know things that could ruin your life.

That was what she said, breezily—and it was an instant, a long instant that felt like a needle that was plunged into my stomach and then quickly extracted. I responded, just as breezily:

—And I have some dirt on you, too. Which is why you'd better toe the line.

We planned to kiss each other on the cheeks, but at the last minute, we both changed our minds and gave each other a light kiss on the lips. I repeated, laughing:

—You be good, now.

5.

That encounter brought a little turbulence to my final days as a bachelor. If, until then, I hadn't even been aware that a stage of my life was about to come to an end, now I began to dig deep and think, uneasily, that in my role as a betrothed man, as a husband, even conjuring up, to myself, the most passionate moments I'd had with those who'd loved and tormented me was now wronged the person who now loved me and made me happy. But I'd be exaggerating if I said that I felt guilty for thinking that I still wanted Teresa. To be honest, what really happened was that, in thinking about her, I recalled an obsession from my childhood that had nothing to do with the erotic realm.

When I was around seven or eight years old, I was often on the verge of jumping out a window. We lived on the fourth floor in those days, and before us lay the countryside, fruit trees, grass, birds, dogs, cats, chicken coops. I'd lock myself up in the bathroom and lean over the narrow windowsill— those times when I was most determined, I'd even sit with my legs dangling over the edge—and look up at the sky that was either blue or grey or full of clouds stretched thin by the wind, and down at the strip of asphalt, the steep path that led to the fields. Most likely I was an unhappy child—rather, I most certainly was—but I don't think I ever really wanted to die. If anything, I was certain that if I jumped, nothing would have happened, not even a broken bone, and that, if anything, I would have been very happy to jump. Nevertheless, even though I was on the verge of leaping out a thousand times, I never did. What made me stop was, I believe, a discrepancy: the absolute certainty of my invulnerability lived side by side, in my mind, with the certainty, just as absolute, that if the bathroom door had suddenly opened wide and someone gave me a playful shove while I was sitting on the windowsill, the challenge would have worn off, and I'd have fallen and died. I never managed to emerge from that contradiction, and the prospect of the prodigious leap lost its sheen. I gave up on it, the way I had given up turning somersaults over an iron rail in the courtyard: one time, a kid I knew slapped me suddenly on the neck, causing me to lose my grip, sending me headfirst to the ground.

This little story from my childhood assumed its place for days, for no reason, next to the adult one with Teresa, and maybe they had sidled up next to each other while she was pulling away on her Vespa and I stood watching her fishing in my pockets for the keys to my Renault. 4. The hours passed and Teresa faded, but the scene of the windowsill, the countryside, and the empty space below didn't dissolve. It haunted me for days like the refrain of a little ditty. Then, right on the heels of the wedding, out of the blue and incongruous as always, practically from within that childhood memory, another thought suddenly popped out: what if Teresa, in one, of her typical flare-ups, if only for the pleasure of pinning me to my responsibilities, tracked down Nadia and told her my secret?

From that moment on I stared to feel awful. I spent a whole day feeling anxious, and that day was followed by a sleepless night. In the morning, to calm down, I decided to call the woman I'd once lived with to remind her, utterly serious, that we had a pact: to never tell anybody, ever, what we'd told one another. I resorted to the number I had, but I discovered that it was no longer active. It was a stroke of fortune; that obstacle forced me to come to my senses. I realized that if I'd spoken to Teresa, she would have done everything in her power to multiply my anxiety; and had I gone on to threaten to reveal her business, in a fit of pique, she would have relished it all the more, replying: up until now I had no intention of shaming you, but now, after what you've said, I most certainly will. So, I let it go, and I got married. Nadia wanted a church wedding, whereas I would have preferred a civil ceremony, but I loved her, as they say, and I was willing to do anything for her. During the ceremony I was afraid, partly kidding myself, but also partly not, that at the perfect moment Teresa would appear and yell out: stop, I must object to this union, I know things I feel obliged to declare publicly. Of course, this didn't happen. In a joyful atmosphere, with no glitch whatsoever, Nadia and I became husband and wife.

6.

The first years of our marriage were in many ways happy. We both worked in the same high school on the outskirts of Rome, and we'd rented, for a song, a lovely apartment in a small building in Montesacro. It belonged to some relatives of

Nadia, who hailed from Protola Peligna, in Abruzzo, along with the rest of her extensive family. We furnished it with care but saying "we" would be to boast; it was my wife who saw to most of it, all I did was arrange the books and a few photos and binders bulging with papers in the chilly room I chose as my study.

It was a cheerful house, the rooms swelled with morning sun and right away we felt at home there. We were in the middle of a garden that radiated intoxicating smells. The earth smelled now of strawberries, now of mushrooms, now of resin, and almost always of damp soil. From the balconies we could see other gardens, and a building from the 1950's that, both in inclement weather and under a clear sky, looked like the outline of an enormous, tranquil beast. On certain mornings the blue sky rested atop a motionless mist that hid the larch trees, and everything seemed miraculously still, as if the traffic roaring toward the ring road were not just a few steps away.

Nadia had gone to university in Naples, where she'd lived until graduating. She spoke of that city fondly, but she didn't love it. Instead, she loved every stone, every leaf of the Peligna Valley, and when she praised the quality of the air—the air of her childhood—it was as if she were praising her very mother, the cheerful teacher at an elementary school who spoke to adults they way she'd always spoken to children. Even when it came to the house in Montesacro, we'd ended up in it not so much because the rent was cheap but because those stones and spaces were linked to her family, so that Nadia felt safe there. Surrounded by nature, she was relieved, given that the oppressive qualities of the city were kept at bay.

I—I must admit it—grew slowly accustomed to the idyll of married life, though I'd never been keen on idylls. When I was a bachelor, at Easter or Christmas, or even on a weekend or a day I didn't have to teach, I couldn't wait to go down to Naples, the city where I'd been born, to the Vasto where I had relatives, friends, and memories from adolescence and childhood. But I also liked staying in Rome, in San Lorenzo, where the studio apartment I'd shared with Teresa was located, and the activities linked to my studies, and political passions, and debates about the state of the planet, and bouts of drinking and poker games, love affairs both flighty and tempestuous. It's not that I didn't like Montesacro, I did, but the way I liked to spend my free time didn't jibe with Nadia's. She loved staying home to study or going for walks along the quiet avenues of our neighborhood, through the city's big villas and their grounds, Villa Torlonia, Villa Borghese, Villa Ada; or better still, taking the car to parts of Abruzzo that she'd known intimately for ages, spending Sundays with her relatives from Pratola, most of all her father, a quiet man who taught science and had been a school principal for many years. So, what can I say? In the beginning, I longed for my bachelor days, but since I liked whatever my wife liked, I soon ended up liking her way of spending time.

Of course, Nadia had immediately picked up on the fact that I was a bit uneasy deep down, and when she heard me on the phone with people I'd perhaps spent time with up until a few years before she'd say: go, they're people you care about, I'm happy if you spend an evening with them, better yet, invite them over, I'd liked to meet them, we have the space, let's throw a party. But I'd always reply, No, I'd rather be with you. And it was true, I loved combining my time with hers, talking about this or that, listening to her while she tried to explain to me the work she'd done for her thesis and what she was still working on thanks to the encouragement of an elderly professor who admired her deeply. But I must admit, I couldn't manage to understand a damn thing about algebraic surfaces, and I'd tell her: I'm a literary nerd who's still stuck on *rosa, rosae, rosae, rosam*—and I confessed that I was ashamed of that. How I wish, Nadia, that I had the kind of mind that could wrap

itself around great literature and, at the same time, great theo-
ries like that of Galileo. But I don't. Nevertheless, I promised
her that I would try my best to understand her subject of study,
because—I whispered, embracing her—I want to know everything there is to know about you, every last thing, and I'd pro-
ceed to kissing her, I was consumed with the desire to smack
my lips over every inch of her skin, tormenting her and making her laugh. She would begin writhing immediately, and
kicked back though she was still, and I threatened her, let me
see what this is, over here, and don't laugh, if you thrash
around like this, I'll end up hurting you to make you feel good,
and meanwhile, with my voice that was as rough as an ogre's,
I'd called her Nigritella, Nigritella Rubra, like the famous
orchid of the Peligna Valley, it was the nickname for a passion
that could never end and for sex that, as soon as it was over,
wanted to start up again.

Meanwhile a very brief article I'd written quite some time
back was published in a triquarterly journal that dealt with
education. I'd never had specific ambitions. My work as a
teacher was enough, and a life full of reading, attention to others, affection. But in Teresa's wake, I'd written out those pages
and, after having set them aside for a while, given them to a
friend to read, someone who knew all about the school system.
I didn't see or hear from this friend for months, until one
morning when a female colleague, quite feisty, whom I'd met
when I'd taken a few run-of-the-mill courses to qualify me to
teach, called me at school to say:

—What have you gone and done?

—No idea, you tell me.

—You've written that public schools are only suited to
those who don't need them.

—Me? That's not true.

—Liar, I have it here, in black and white. And I'm not the
only one who's angry. We all are. We're writing a letter now, to

say that a serious journal should never had published such a superficial article.

—You've misread it, I was speaking in general terms. I wasn't alluding to teachers like you.

The public life of the essay I'd written began with that painful phone call, to the extent that I never bought the journal and I avoided talking about it with Nadia, and I even quickly forgot about the essay and about the phone call. Instead, I bought the subsequent issue because my friend got in touch and announced, cheerfully refusing to be more explicit, that in the issue that had just been released, I'd find a pleasant surprise. The editors—I discovered—had published the letter of complaint, which wasn't so ferocious after all, rather, it was written in calm language and was sensibly argued. But—and this was the surprise—the letter was boxed inside a much longer piece, signed by a well-known pedagogue at the time, Stefano Itrò, who praised my little article in no uncertain terms, maybe even to excess.

When I read the two pieces to Nadia, in the kitchen, while outside—I recall—the cold felt Siberian, and the wind struck our little house, extracting terrifying sounds from within its walls, she asked:

—Why didn't you ever mention it to me?

—What?

—Your essay.

—I wrote it before we got together.

—But you never mentioned it now that we're married, either.

—It didn't seem important. You work on things that are actually serious. I wrote a trifling thing.

—Did she read it back then?

—Who's she?

—The woman you were with before me.

—Teresa? No, we'd already split up.

—I tell you all about my aspirations. You say nothing.

—I'll go grab it and read you the whole thing out loud. You'll see it's not worth it.

The reply, unlike our typically polite exchanges, was harsh:

—If it's not worth it, then don't waste my time.

After a few days I understood why she was so tense. That very same morning she'd gone to the lab to drop off some urine to see if she was pregnant. She'd done it without telling me, those were days when women like Nadia (not Teresa who, every time her period vaguely tarried, said, are you sure you haven't pulled a fast one on me?) skipped, slightly embarrassed, over certain manifestations of their bodies. One afternoon I came home after a boring meeting at school and saw that she was happy. She was officially pregnant, and she no longer cared about the fact that I hadn't told her about my essay.

7.

The nine months of her pregnancy flew by. My wife didn't suffer much from morning sickness, she vomited discreetly, and it was with the same discretion, with gritted teeth, that she faced the labor and delivery. In a few short days she was on her feet again, pretending even to herself that not only had it not been painful, but that she was free of any aftereffects. And so I found Emma, my first daughter, in my arms—a purplish, finely-crafted little idol—not as if she'd been expelled by Nadia, who was obeying the impulses of her own body, but as if she'd really been brought, sweetly, by the stork.

I was incredibly proud. I'd turned thirty with flying colors, I liked my job, I was married and adored my wife, and I held in my arms the perfect reproduction of a living female body to whose creation I'd contributed as much as I possibly could. In addition, thanks to that essay of mine, for the past few months I was being invited, now and then, to give talks about the school system. But that wasn't all. The very day that Emma turned six months old, I got a phone call from a reputable publisher. An emphatic woman's voice, probably an efficient secretary who had no time to waste, said:

—My name is Tilde Pacini, may I transfer you to Professor Itrò?

I felt a blaze of astonishment in my chest, as if, while lighting the gas under the espresso pot one fine morning, I felt my pajamas catching on fire. Professor Itrò was the pedagogue who had written that fulsome elegy to my essay, and upon hearing his name I could barely contain myself: I emitted a guttural noise, a sort of wild, enthusiastic *whoa*. Tilde asked:

—I didn't catch that, Sir. Sorry, are you busy?

—Not at all, please put him on, thanks.

Itrò, after asking a few questions about where I taught, and what, and since when, suggested that I transform my essay into a short book for a series that he edited.

—A hundred pages, he said.

—That's impossible. It's too much, I'll never be able to write so many pages.

—You'll end up writing three hundred that you'll have to cut down.

—Can I think about it?

—For as long as you like.

This time I talked to Nadia about it right away, and at first she was happy—how wonderful she said, twice, her eyes looking tired—but then two minutes later she looked worried.

—How will we manage?

—What do you mean?

—How will we manage with Emma? I can't keep asking my mother or my sister to help out.

—I'll write at night, when she's sleeping

—Will you need to do much away from home?

—I doubt it.

—Because I need to go down to Naples, otherwise the University gets upset.

—Of course.

I called Tilde Pacini, I told her yes, and two weeks later I received a contract to sign. I'd have had no problem signing it right away and sending it back to the publisher, but Nadia wanted to look it over carefully. She read it and reread it, scouring the codicils for signs that might threaten our life as a couple, and as a result our daughter, but all she learned was that the advance, by all definitions a pittance, was too low. I was grateful for her efforts, I kissed her all over and explained that for me that book was largely something to pass the time, to practice my penmanship. And so she finally let me sign it, even though she was like some Penelope who, in vain, warns Odysseus, should he meet the Sirens, to plug his ears with wax and think only of Telemachus' future.

I wrote the book in very little time. It didn't get over eighty pages. It was hard to manage Emma's needs, Nadia who had to go down to Naples to see her professor, and my needing to get to the library for my research. But Nadia's mother helped us out quite a bit, and Nadia sacrificed a bit more than she usually did, and I handed in my book exactly on time.

I took it over to the publisher myself, and on that occasion, I met Tilde. She was a woman in her forties with a lovely, intelligent face, the kind with very fine bone structure, small almond-shaped eyes under short blonde hair, and a long neck that rose up like a stalk from a dress of soft blue wool. I also saw Itrò, nearing his sixties, short, very thin, with watchful eyes, as if he were afraid of being ambushed every time he walked down a hallway, every time he opened a door. I went to lunch with both of them, to a nice restaurant by the Pantheon, and they treated me kindly. A week later that kindness had morphed into excitement. Tilde told me cheerfully on the phone: great news, that's all I'll say for now. Come by our offices tomorrow at four o'clock.

I headed over with nearly an hour to spare, and spent it wandering around the building, pleasantly agitated. Upon greeting me Itrò said that the book had surpassed his expectations, and that I'd done a fantastic job. Tilde—who, I discovered that day, was not a secretary but an editor—spoke in more modulated tones.

—You—she told me—really are honest. Honest and also naive, a precious combination that's the sign of a free man.

—Thank you.

—We need to work on it a bit, nothing serious, the book's all there.

—All right, whatever you say.

We worked on it for a couple of months. I went to the publishers twice a week, throwing Nadia's finely tuned organization of time out of whack. But it was a necessary thwacking. Tilde double-checked all my statements, all my citations, even the rare statistics I incorporated here and there, and so I found quite a few discrepancies in my argument, and a few bibliographic errors, and even an embarrassing spelling mistake. I got to know her pretty well. She was smart but funny. We realized we had quite a few friends in common, people in their thirties and forties, all people committed to bettering the world and, as a result, bettering the school system. It turned out that I'd even had some connection with her husband, long ago. He remembered me. I didn't remember him but said I did.

—Do you often make that sound? she asked once when, given that we were by then friends, we took a break together, sipping coffees in a squalid hallway at the publishing house.

—Which?

She made a silly sound, and for a few seconds she abruptly turned from the composed, reserved lady that she was into a lovely young girl who made funny faces.

—Whooa.

—No, I only did it that once.

—Please do it again.

—Whoa.

She tapped me lightly on the cheek.

—Yes, you really are a good person.

Itrò turned up then and joined the conversation, and without any clear referent, with his subtle voice, that of a highly educated gentleman, asked:

—Do you have a wife?

—Yes.

—And what does she do?

—She teaches in the same school, that's where we met. But she also works in the math department at the University of Naples, she's brilliant.

—Great, we'll ask her to write a book for us, too. Tell her that.

—Yes, Tilde said. On the teaching of the sciences. The twin of what you've done.

—We have a daughter who's less than a year old. She takes up all our time.

—We'll ask the baby for a book, too, Itrò quipped.

8.

As far back as I could remember I'd never liked myself, not as a child, not as an adult. But that afternoon I started to think, as I returned to Montesacro on the bus, that the conjunction of diverse circumstances—the breakup with Teresa, the painful aftermath at the end of a love affair that I'd survived by writing a brief, well-received essay, the marriage to Nadia, Emma's birth, and now that book, along with the warm welcome of a person as highly regarded as Itrò and a woman as competent as Tilde—meant that I was taking a turn for the better. There was one thing, however, that I didn't care for in that list. The bus was moving down the shadowy stretch of Via Nomentana beneath pellets of rain that were shearing the long leaves of the plane trees, blackened with smog, when I realized that among the positive events that had taken place in my life in recent years, I'd included the breakup with Teresa. In that moment it seemed mean of me. The worst of our relationship had by now turned to ashes that, observed from a distance, revealed a faint design on the surface, bearable on the whole. And since it had been a while that we no longer tormented each other, the time we'd spent enjoying one another felt marvelously rich and intense. As I was walking home from the bus stop, battling with the umbrella that the wind, with sudden gusts mixed with rain, kept shifting from a cupola into a cup—how easy it is for words to change the shape of things—I thought: who knows where she ended up, what she does, I must look her up, write to her, tell her the great news about the book, and about how things were changing for me.

But when I got home Teresa slipped from my mind. I found the apartment in disarray, Emma crying, Nadia on edge. I set myself at once to reassuring my wife, trying to make her laugh and to calm Emma at the same time, giving her the baby food she didn't want from her mother, making little jokes and funny faces all the while. Finally, we had dinner, and I washed up the dishes while entertaining Emma, who drooled in her highchair. I wanted to put her to bed, even though she never wanted to go to sleep with me because I liked to see her happy and kept playing with her. After that I went to Nadia, who had begun, sullenly, to study. I told her about the afternoon at the publishers and that the book would go to press soon. I kissed her neck and whispered:

—Let's go to bed, Nigritella.

—You go. I have work to do, and if you keep talking to me about your day, I'll be up all night long.

—Can't you work tomorrow morning and be in my arms for a while?

—If I keep procrastinating, I'll never do any work.

I realized she was about to burst into tears and said quickly:

—I really have finished working on the book. From now on I'll take care of everything.

—There you go again.

—You know I will. And I have to introduce you to Itrò, and also to Tilde Pacini. They're wonderful people.

She swallowed her tears.

—Lovers?

—Of course not. He's married with four kids. And Tilde's married, too. Her husband's a great guy, I knew him at university. They have two children, an eight-year-old and a twelve-year-old.

—Let's have them over to dinner.

—Yes, I'd like to invite both Tilde and Itrò. He'd like to have you write a book along the same lines as mine but focused on the sciences.

I thought the idea would please her, but instead Nadia turned suddenly sullen again. This time, dry-eyed, she said:

—You know that I've been working for years on something that will determine my future at the university?

I nodded without replying. I left her to her work and went to bed.

9.

The next day I called a girlfriend Teresa had lived with before moving in with me to the studio in San Lorenzo. She was the one who told me that Teresa, with one of her unpredictable maneuvers, had left Wisconsin, landed at MIT, and was now living in Boston. This friend didn't know either when or why that change of institution and prospects had taken place: needless to say—she said—she was always brilliant and now she's doing something important, so much so that I saw her name in a prestigious science magazine in America that listed promising young scientists from all over the world.

That news didn't make me happy, on the contrary, it upset me. I'd called to find out about Teresa and above all to obtain an address so that I could write to her. I'd done this without putting too much stock in it (if she knows where I can write her, well and good, if not, oh well). But as soon as I'd made my request I noticed that the friend, who surely had the address, wasn't willing to give it to me. To justify myself, I said something along the lines of: love fades, but friendship endures, and I ended up saying that I wanted to send her a book of mine that was soon to be published. So the friend finally gave me the address, but I sensed that she feared she'd made a mistake.

As soon as I got off the phone, I realized that I was even more anxious and that I no longer felt like writing to Teresa. What would I say to her, what was the point of telling her about my essay about the school system? She was in the United States, she was at MIT, god only knew what amazing work she was accomplishing. Maybe she'd forgotten all about me, maybe she, too, had gotten married, or maybe, in that carefree way of hers, without commitment, she lived with some scientist no less promising. And above all I knew her well: Teresa tended to be brilliantly, creatively perfidious; her perfidy, typically, didn't work in the shadows, with coded language for those who might understand, but was blurted outright into the faces of those who were its object, with a burst of intelligence that ended up entertaining those present and also the victim himself; so forget about what she might be capable of in a moment of triumph, in her absolute prime. I feared that she would destroy my feeble state of well-being, and I left the slip of paper with her address at school, in my locker, dedicating myself to the role of the person, according to Tilde, honest to the point of being ingenuous, and thus free. And that was exactly what I wanted to be.

But that spell of anxiety never fully broke. One morning I thought back to the phone call with Teresa's friend. I'd asked, do you have an address, I'd like to write her, and immediately on the heels of my question came that fraction of a second when the person you're talking to wavers between the truth on the tip of her tongue and the lie she's about to cobble together in a hurry. There might have been a hundred different explanations for that infinitesimal fragment of perplexed silence, but the important thing here is that whatever the reason, I thought: maybe Teresa told her something unpleasant about me, and that's the reason she's hesitating.

This scenario transformed by anxiety into actual worry, even into fear. Was it possible that Teresa had told her friend what I'd confided in her? No—I tried to calm myself down— that's impossible, she has a thousand flaws but she's not a gossip, she doesn't talk behind people's backs, if she promises to keep something to herself, she will. And yet I was unable to calm down and I got hold of the address again. Now it wasn't out of friendship that I wanted to write her, but because I felt her distant and beyond my control, like a comet that leaves a foul trail in its wake. I hoped the letter would have brought me closer to her, also that it would have provided a means to determine whether or not she wanted to damage me. My book was about to come out. Tilde and Itrò believed that it was the written proof of my professional and personal attributes. All I needed was for some nasty rumor to start circulating around me. I scribbled down the letter, and the first three or four pages emerged with the usual light humor. After congratulating her for what I called her American triumphs, after telling her about Emma's birth and my piddling affairs in Italy, after talking exhaustively about how life turned some people better and others worse, after having emphasized that she and I belonged to the first category—in fact, we were both working to our fullest capacity—I wrote in the end: good thing we broke up, it was the only way to keep caring for each other. Hugs, kisses, and I sent off the letter just as, when walking down a lonely path in the mountains or in the countryside, you nod in a friendly way at a stranger and await a similar, reassuring nod.

After that I felt relieved. I took it for granted that she'd reply in her disenchanted way, something along the lines of: My Dear, I never cared deeply for you, but given that you're behaving responsibly, I can start now, sure. But if truth be told, I hoped for something else, some sort of explicit renewal of our secret pact. A considerable part of me feared that the dam would burst and that the despicable part of me would spread. I wanted Teresa to tell me: the dam still holds, you idiot, there's no danger.

10.

I waited for weeks. The response never came. I began to worry again, but I was so obviously worried for no reason that in the end I forgot what I was even worried about. Especially since I soon had other things to think about. My little book appeared on the shelves of bookstores. Tilde had great contacts with newspaper editors, not to mention that Stefano Itrò's name meant a lot in those days, a guarantee of quality. Within a month, they both saw to it that reviews began to come out here and there, reviews which, even when they spoke critically about the book, lavishly praised its merits. It thrilled me to read them one after the next, most of all because not only people who knew me and liked me but also reviewers, whom I'd never met in my life, seemed to imagine me as the kind of person I was finally managing to become. Both those who praised my pages and those who found fault ended up, always, by calling me rigorous, cultured, at times disenchanted, never disaffected.

Tilde was pleased. She summed up, solemnly, in a way I'd never heard her speak (she was a woman who abhorred effusive speech): they're recognizing your fundamental traits: a noble heart and a subtle intelligence. Itrò himself pored over the reviews and concluded: I think the general public will also welcome you warmly. But in the beginning that prediction was inaccurate. Tilde set up a presentation at the Feltrinelli in Via del Babuino. She brought together a pedagogue no less famous than Itrò, a hard-hitting school principal, a teacher who was on the dull side, and a student—a classic grind—who all talked too long in front of forty-odd people, including colleagues who had come from my high school for the occasion, a few of my dedicated students, Nadia with her relatives, and of course Emma, who cried out all the while because she wanted to come into my arms to play just as I was saying a few clumsy words about why I'd written the book. We talked amongst ourselves, so much so that there was no time for questions. The only one who got a word in was a thickset guy with thin lips and a forehead that overwhelmed his face. He said: if this book becomes popular, then we're not going to be able to talk seriously about the school system for a long time, and then he up and left as the panelists and the audience members all looked uncomfortable. Good thing Nadia and Emma made an excellent impression on Tilde and Itrò. Each of them in their separate ways told me: why have you kept such a beautiful, intelligent wife, such an enchanting child, hidden away?

Nadia, too, seemed happy to meet them, and when we were back home she spoke of them warmly. In bed, before turning off the lights, she consoled me for the harsh feedback from the guy with the thin lips. She said: you have no idea how much that enraged me, what a loathsome creature, I'd have slapped him in the face; but good thing you kept your cool, you really are a good person, you know. She concluded: let's hold on tightly to our life together, please, that's all that matters.

I told her she was right, but I struggled to fall asleep. For at least an hour, I turned over possible fierce replies to the rude things that stranger said, and I struggled in vain to fend off Teresa, who shouted out cheerfully from MIT: My Dear, you're getting upset with the only person who had a critical eye. Nevertheless, the next day, I felt better. I'd written my book sincerely, I was still doing a good job as a teacher, and the family dynamics, for better or for worse, were proceeding apace. I hugged Nadia, who was still sleeping, and given that it had been hard for her, in recent weeks, to see her old cantankerous professor, I encouraged her to take advantage of her day off from school and go down to Naples, to face up to that illustrious man, and ask him to talk to her in no uncertain terms about her academic future. I took Emma to work and entrusted her to one of my students. I taught the male members of the class while the females pretended to listen but played with the baby instead. When I left, I bought an album so that I could save all the reviews, and in the afternoon, I placed them under cellophane sheets with Emma playfully assisting me. I also organized, on the shelves of my chilly study, my three author's copies, thus mentally closing that discreet episode of my life.

My wife retuned in the evening, exhausted, her face drained of color. She said the same thing pretty much that I'd said to myself about me and my book, but in a more dramatic way: "My days at that university are over, the professor hasn't read even a page of what I sent him over a month ago, or more likely, he's read them, of course he's read them, and he's realized that I'm not cut out for serious research." I tried to lift her spirits, I asked her to tell me exactly what the professor had said, and I grasped feebly at utterances in order to convince her that she was exaggerating, that she was in fact greatly respected, that soon enough the old man would really look at her equations, and so forth, and that everything would right itself.

That was what I sincerely hoped would happen to her. But things went in a different direction, and my situation was the one that improved. Tilde called me often to tell me about a new review, that we had an invitation from a bookstore, from a high school, that a few conferences had asked about me, in brief, that the book was generating interest and making the rounds. Disoriented, a bit anxious, I found myself encountering my readers, as they say: people who had forked over money to be able to read me and who, now, even wanted to engage in conversation with me.

—Are you saying that, under present circumstances, it's no longer possible ever to do a good job?

—Yes.

—So we should shut down the schools?

—No.

—Well then?

—Inequality is the issue.

—How so?

—If you have a number of natural and social privileges, but I don't have any, how can school raise both of us to the same level, given that it treats us as equals?

At the start I'd clear my throat, I'd say nothing, I'd grow flustered. I was ill at ease: apart from my teaching, I almost never spoke in public. Sure, once in a while I had to say a few words at a teachers' meeting or at a student assembly, which were moments of tense debate back then, and I must admit, I was never very capable. But I slowly learned that, when I talked about my book, after working past the initial discomfort, I felt as if I were in class talking about, let's say, Quintilian or Cicero. In fact, such was the desire to obtain and maintain the audience's attention, to discern that it was both receptive and at the same time reactive, that I ended up not only convincing them but winning them over. I knew, with oral exposition, how to improve the very qualities in my writing, and when a naysayer like that guy in Rome turned up, or those unavoidable guardians of the party line in school politics—clones, in each syllable and modulation of voice, of the colleague who, back then, had made that threatening call—I managed to volley back with a well-mannered irony that people appreciated.

In keeping with my school hours, I often went on the road, at the start mostly in small towns in Abruzzo, thanks to the friendships made by Nadia's parents and relatives, who were all teachers and professors for several generations. I was learning the ropes, I never knew exactly what I was going to say, and I'd toss out whatever came to mind. Now and then, someone would get annoyed:

—So you're opposed to the top students, the ones at the top of the class, the few that really study?

—No.

—That's what you just said.

—All I was trying to say was that the more the students repeat what we say, word for word, the more we tend to think they're smart.

—And aren't they?

—Of course they are. But we run the risk of being dazzled by those in our likeness, and not appreciating people who are bright in ways other than our own.

—What are you saying?

—My friend, if I recognize my cultured bourgeois norms in you and give you great marks, there's the danger that I don't take into account or that I even penalize all those who don't subscribe to my mediocre intelligence.

It often went around like this, in circles. But over time, I learned that certain formulas worked well, and I learned to hold onto them, to memorize them—I should keep this one in store—to hone them, to repeat them as soon as the occasion presented itself. When, for instance, I'd say that my only objective, from the first day I started teaching, had been: try to do your job such that you won't damage your pupils the way your teachers damaged you, nearly everyone present got excited, as if on cue. And as a result, I was careful at every gathering to usher the conversation to the place where remarks of that variety could be unleashed to their greatest potential.

—When you started to teach, what principles did you base your work on?

—None that I can think of.

—Did one of your teachers serve as a model?

—My teachers? No, absolutely not. On the contrary, my only objective was: don't damage your pupils the way your teachers damaged you.

I'd say things like that with a sense of ironic pleasure, and my repertoire quickly expanded. We teachers were turned into prisoners by our schools when we were six years old and never set free. Don't let power teach you, you should be the ones to teach power. A good education creates community, not a clique. It's not about teaching the happy few well, but teaching the unhappy many just as well. You learn more from the outsider than from members of your own clan. Etcetera, slogans like this. They were flowers that I let suddenly bloom in the grey gardens of the public school debate. They were bits of gold that I'd carefully worked so that they glimmered in the dark, depressing spheres of scholastic conversations. The invitations doubled, and tripled, and I started to travel not just to Abruzzo and to the outskirts of Rome but all over Italy. The events were usually organized by penniless groups of radicals heartily committed to union politics. So, all of it was on a shoestring, I swallowed down sandwiches and slept at the home of the person who'd organized the event. I'd step into unknown apartments in the middle of the night and leave first thing in the morning, to hop on a bus or a train or a car, to go back home or straight to school.

The situation saddened Nadia, and turned Emma extremely fussy. I was either at school or on the road, and my absence, I quickly understood, wasn't appreciated by my wife as a promotional necessity but as a sneaky way to shirk off my family responsibilities. The resentments piled up, and things got complicated when she went down to Naples for the umpteenth time and came back late at night, got into bed without saying a word to me, and lay there, motionless, all night long. It was impossible, for days, to get her to tell me what had happened. When she decided to talk to me—her face was extremely pale—she said:

—I'm done with the University.

—That's what you always say.

—This time I mean it.

—Why?

—That's my business.

—Your business is my business.

—No. Each person minds his or her own business. They're categories that are, inevitably, quite separate. Please don't ask me any more questions.

11.

It's so hard to have truly clear communication when you're in a couple. I loved Nadia, I wanted to help her, but I didn't love her to the point of forcing her to tell me what had happened at the university, what had distanced her forever from algebraic surfaces. My questions had always been meek, because I sensed that if she were to uncork her rage and dismay and disgust and who knows what else that, with admirable self-control, she'd shoved into some recess of her brain, we'd be at it for a while. It would have lasted from day into night and into the day after that: quarrels, fights, migraines, tears, soul searching, childhood memories, adolescence, adult frailties, advice to carry on, in short, an ongoing wave that would have crashed over me. I'd no longer be able to honor the thousands of commitments I'd taken on: teaching, public talks, travels, reflections, my studies, the obligatory hours with Emma, the walks with the stroller but also without, given that our daughter now walked on her own, and also ran, and no longer babbled but spoke in sentences.

Clearing the air when you're in a couple, well, whatever that means. Perhaps it's necessary, but perhaps it's also a dangerous indulgence. Doing so might have upset both Nadia and me a great deal, and I was in a phase of enjoying life like never before, especially when I hopped on a train and arrived in a city I'd never been in and talked to people I'd never meet again. Meanwhile, the press's publicity department had started to ramp up its efforts; they'd moved on to a prudent handling of the invitations and now aimed at occasions that would raise my profile. At times Itrò would accompany me, and he and I would speak to a tightly packed, discerning audience, given that his authority radiated automatically toward me and my book, and the evening would conclude with dinner with a group of stuffy and influential people. On other occasions, Tilde would go with me, and I'd have to give it my all—she communicated in brief sentences, fussing with her hands, her fingers stacked with rings—the thin wedding band and a few others with precious stones—and after five minutes she finished and it would be my turn to talk. On those trips, I was struck by the amount

of luggage she carried: elegant travel clothes, elegant presentation clothes, elegant clothes for going out to dinner with the
people who'd organized the event. The dinners were as boring
as the ones with Itrò's distinguished friends, but Tilde insisted
on good wine, and we made it a rule to order different dishes
so that we could trade halfway through, and we spoke often
just the two of us, ignoring our hosts and continuing to talk
even after they'd peeled off. What we said to one another until
late at night is useless for me to summarize here; they were
complicated conversations but there was also some random
chitchat. The point being that we laughed a lot, for no particular reason, and that I'd let her taste the calamari, extending
my fork to her, and she'd give me a taste of her soup, directing
the spoon toward me as if I were an invalid.

Since the age of seventeen, I knew that the exchange of
those words, foods, and bits of spittle paved the way for
exchanges of another variety, but in that particular case I was
certain: ours was a sibling-like bond, and if perhaps there was
some incestuous element, it would never go beyond an educated, metaphorical exercise.

Except that one morning, in a hotel in Florence, before
heading back by car to Rome, at the end of a breakfast that was
already in and of itself excessive, I was about to dig into yet
another generous slice of a buttery chocolate concoction that
I'd snatched from the buffet table.

—Should we split it? I asked Tilde.

—No way, I'm about to burst.

—Me too. But it's a pity. I'll just have a bite.

The fork was sullied by an excellent cheese, and the spoon
had traces of fig jam. Without thinking, I stuck my thumb,
pointer, and middle finger into the slice of cake, pried off big
chunk, and raised it toward my mouth. There was just a bit of
it left between my fingers. Delicious, I said, and was about to
eat that, too, when Tilde, laughing, grabbed my wrist and said:

I've changed my mind, give me a bite. And I extended my arm, she leaned forward, and her mouth welcomed not only the piece of cake but my fingers as well, which she squeezed between her lips for a fraction of a second, grazing them with her tongue. I got my lipstick on you, she said after that, and I looked at my fingers and told her she hadn't.

In the past, before meeting Nadia and marrying her, an encounter like that, early in the morning, would have set flame to the fantasy, and I'd have schemed to get Tilde up to my room straightaway, into the bed where I'd just woken. Whereas now I noticed that her eyes were red from too little sleep, and that her complexion was a bit sallow, her nose shiny with perspiration, and it occurred to me that she was making an effort—at ten minutes to eight, before getting into the car to drive back down to Rome—simply to be pleasant company. The night before, we'd stayed up late, she'd told me that she was worried about her daughters, who were left to their own devices, that she and her husband both worked too much and spent too little time together, that it was a pity one's energy dwindled, because it was really when you started to get closer to your forties that life turned clamorous, that it darted from one thing to the next, that it started to covet all that could be coveted. But she—mostly she, her husband less—was too tired to covet anything, tired in her thoughts, and at times—at this point her eyes suddenly gleamed with tears—she wished she could sleep for a whole year. Fat chance she's in the mood for sex, I thought. All I need now is to make the wrong move and ruin her opinion of me. And so each of us returned to our separate rooms, and ten minutes after that we met downstairs with our suitcases, and left. As she drove toward Rome, she made a point, more than once, of talking about my candor. I want to be your friend, she said. You're subversive but candid, you're smart but transparent. Oh, how those definitions thrilled me; I'd always wanted people to describe me in those terms. I returned home burnt out from the trip, but happy.

—Maybe—Nadia said—I can't remember if it was that same night or the next one—you need to spend a little more time dealing with Emma.

—Sure.

—Enough, then, with all this coming and going.

—I'm in demand, the book's doing really well.

—But you don't always have to say yes. Are you a pedagogue? Are you a sociologist who's made a formal investigation of some kind? Have you written a history of Italian schools? No. You're the author of a single, short essay that you yourself—I'll remind you—called a trifle, ever since it was first published in a little magazine, and you even told me to not waste my time reading it. So why are you pouring so much time and energy into this foolish endeavor, and hardly any to our daughter?

At this point I must pause for a moment to draw attention to the fact that, in that moment, I totally gave in to the truth of a cliché. I thought: we fall in love with people who seem real, but don't really exist. We invent them. I don't know this self-assured woman, who speaks to me in such clipped sentences, this fearless, scathing woman. She's not Nadia. There's the person we love and then there's the real person, but as long as we love the person, we never see the real person underneath. We inevitably waste so much time, I said to myself, loving people. These past few years, I happily invented a person. I've taken great pleasure entering into the body of a pale watercolor of my own making, and in the other room, I have a real daughter that my own invention gave birth to. Thinking along those lines, I felt tragically solemn, in keeping with my ideas of a man who views life with clarity. Those words of Nadia's had been so incredibly harsh. I felt my blood surge, and everything inside me started to roil like an earthquake. The words rattled in my head, first in whispers, then shouting, and they assumed a speed that shredded them, that reduced them to separate syllables, then to an animal that snarls: Nadia, I'm a cultured man, I read, I study, I don't need a university title to express ideas that—and listen up here—only I can call a trifle with intentional modesty, you, no, you have to study them the way you studied—obtusely, in vain—your algebraic surfaces; quite to the contrary, you have to study them better, and above all, you need to talk about them with respect, without ever daring to tell me when and how I should spend my time, where and when I should be with my daughter, when and how I need to feed her and give her the pacifier and her grated apple along with the banana, because I'm not one to be bossed around by anyone, especially someone who talks to her daughter sounding like a complete idiot: Emma is a normal kid, and it's useless and damaging that, instead of saying, Emma, would you like a drink, you ask her, in that chirpy voice, what does this little girl want from mommy, does she want a drinky-winky? Because, and I'll say this just once, if you keep talking like that, I'll kick you out of my life, just like they kicked you out of the math department, got that?

But while that monologue was shrieking inside my head, something evidently must have been shrieking outside, too—shards, fragments, who knows what—I hoped little or nothing—because, as usual, Nadia started to cry, mumbling: let go of my arm, you're hurting me. And I was scared, I couldn't bear the idea of hurting anyone. I apologized, dried her tears with kisses, called her Nigritella Rubra. I had to resort to every jest in my repertoire. She withdrew, sent me away, then surrendered to my embraces as she sobbed. She was worn out, depressed. Before she fell asleep, she asked quietly:

—Have you gotten back in touch with your ex?

In touch? Ex?

—Sleep, I whispered.

She sank into sleep, then shuddered awake, turning her shoulders to me and muttering:

—I put the letter on your desk.

So Teresa had written back. I waited for Nadia to fall asleep, I got up, praying the bed wouldn't creak, and I went to my study. So, she'd finally deigned to get in touch. But on the sheet of paper, there were only a few letters of the alphabet, and they ended with a question mark: You're scared, huh?

12.

I'd always been a bit of a perfectionist, which was probably why I never liked myself. I wanted to be irreproachable, but given that in any situation there was always someone with good reason to reproach me, I grew up dissatisfied with who I was, and afraid of being blamed for something or other. On the other hand, I had a lively disposition, at times I was even cheerful and curious about the world, such that I'd never fallen into a melancholic slump, and the fact of not liking myself never prevented me from attempting to please. And so I was accustomed to a precarious balance between what I would have liked to be—to wit, irreproachable—and feeling resigned to my inadequacies, to ensuing objections, and to critics, whom I generally confronted with half smiles, self-mockery, and the amused ease of someone who says: I screwed up, but let's keep it in perspective, it's not a tragedy.

In truth it was a total facade. I never took anything lightly, even things that were light in their very nature. On certain occasions—fortunately, very rare ones—it so happened that something broke inside me. Six years ago, for example, after the grueling evaluations at the end of the year, a colleague had noticed that I'd forgotten to copy down god knows what, and attacked me publicly, shouting that because of my absentmindedness, we'd have to start all over again. True, it was my fault, but I couldn't manage to keep things in perspective by resorting to the usual wordplay. I went apeshit, and I, too, started shouting: yes, I screwed up, and I'll screw up again, because I don't know what I'm doing, because I don't give a fuck about what we're doing, because I have zero attention span, because I'm not capable, because you've all been a royal pain in the ass, and I'd like to see each of you burn in the middle of your goddamn paperwork. But while I was yelling, my voice, greatly ashamed, began to lose its force, and turned high-pitched, humiliating me, and I felt tears filling my eyes. Everyone present, including my obnoxious colleague, immediately quieted down. It's not a big deal, someone said then—above all the more maternal of my colleagues—it will all get sorted out, we'll handle it, if you're tired, take a break, go smoke a cigarette. I turned on my heels, leaving them there, and went to the courtyard to have a smoke. I was furious with them because they knew how to play the role, and with myself because I'd revealed that I was inadequate. Therefore no, I'd say no, I didn't tolerate errors, I didn't tolerate the consequences of errors, I didn't tolerate having to make excuses, I didn't tolerate anything that made me reckon with the fact that I wasn't capable of being perfect, and that I never would be.

By the time Teresa and I had broken up, I understood with great clarity that I hadn't established my life on the basis of great ambitions merely because, if I was imperfect in the piddling matters of a piddling life, how in the world would I handle important matters of an important life? My father was an electrical technician, and in the course of his extremely tiring life, the poor man set himself to turning me into the amazing person that would teach a brilliant lesson to all the people who lorded over him and humiliated him. He'd say, when he got terminally ill: you need to resurrect me, Pietrí, because I need to be there, with my eyes wide open, that very moment when you fuck all those people who thought they were better than me up their ass. But the great expectations of that embittered man had induced me early on, driven by my own insecurity, to mar myself with discreet peccadillos. And I fear that he knew about my flub-ups for a while, because I, too, hoped that he'd know about them. Once, when I was almost seventeen, I'd purposefully bragged, in front of him, that I'd slept with the wife of one of his cousins. I did this because my father was a person repulsed by adultery more than anything else; he loathed infidelity both on the part of the seducers and those seduced, and so I wanted him to grow indignant and raise the great weight of his hypercritical judgment over my head. And in fact, he said, with eyes narrowed in disgust: is it possible that I've got a son who's an even bigger shithead than all the other shitheads? And I, on the verge of tears, (but I didn't cry, I never cry) thought: it's possible, papà, it's extremely possible. But now things were proceeding in such a way that, who knows, maybe he'd have been happy. Every move was successful, that age-old weight was lifting, maybe I really did know how to be irreproachable. It was therefore unbearable that everything was jamming up at the very moment in which I found myself on the right path. Nadia, the person who had probably reorganized me body and soul by loving me, now wanted to pull me down? Teresa, the person who had set that need for reorganization in motion, tormenting me, was threatening me from Boston with the words: You're scared, huh? Which of them should I be more afraid of?

I knew right away that I could cope with my wife, but not with Teresa. Nadia, as she slept, her face still flushed from tears, was slowly complying again with the rules of amorous fiction. She was once again the young adored woman who, certainly, might backslide now and then because her career aspirations had gone nowhere, because she was a tired, anxious mother; but that soft smooth female body, tamed with love for me, remained. Teresa, on the other hand, hadn't loved me for quite some time, Teresa had retreated, darting away from me thanks to an animal instinct with which, moreover, I too had retreated from her. Teresa, for the sole pleasure of an intellectual game, could damage me. She was the one I had to appease.

But one afternoon—in my little room, while I turned that sheet of nearly entirely blank paper in my hands, one she'd sent me from a land I'd never visited, and perhaps never would—I sensed that there was something off about that scheme. I thought about the attention I owed Nadia, the cautious way I had to present myself to her, so as not to irritate her and not to have to contend with the woman she really was. And for the first time in four years—and, if memory serves me, also the last—I feared I'd made a mistake. I shouldn't have allowed things with Teresa to fall apart at the very moment when we'd mutually revealed not only who we really were, free from all staging, but had also revealed, one to the other, who, had the occasion arisen, we might have been. With Nadia, I thought, who knows how much time I'll have to lose in hiding myself and her hiding herself to me, thereby saving our relationship and the family we'd created; with Teresa there's no wasting time, we know much more about each other than people should rightfully know. And so there was no point beating around the bush, if anything, better to face off directly.

I sat down to respond to those three words—You're scared, huh?—with a long, melancholy letter in which I went back over the key points in our relationship. I declared that I'd always cared for her the way one cares for a person held in highest regard, and I kept repeating the following idea: I'm hardly scared, Teresa, I know you like I know no other person, and I trust you just as much as you know that you can trust me. It goes without saying that I sent off the letter without expecting a reply. All I wanted was for her, too, to realize how precious, in its rarity, our relationship was. So direct, without any fear of appearances, given that the essence had already been seen.

13.

Time went by and the interest in my book died down, so I traveled less through Italy. I didn't mind this, I went back to my teaching and took care of Emma. But I sensed that it was mostly my wife who needed attention. She was stunned that I'd resigned myself to going back to life as usual without grumbling about it. She was on edge, and I felt like she was spying on me. She behaved as if she sought to predict my intentions before I did, intentions I was unaware of even having at the time.

—No plans this week?

—No, they've stopped calling.

—Then we can take Emma up to my parents' this Saturday.

—Sure.

—Are you depressed?

—What are you talking about?

—Did you just think of something terrible?

—I don't think so.

For a while I thought that she, fixated on my book and on its success, hadn't realized how much my general condition had improved. I'd become a public figure, sure, a minor one, but one with a certain authority, nevertheless. My views—I myself struggled to believe this—had doubled or perhaps even tripled in weight, to the degree that now and then a journalist would call me on the phone to ask my opinion on some scholastic matter. Tilde, a highly cultured and elegant woman—that was another atmosphere, another world—called me almost every day, and we exchanged thoughts and speculated about a new essay I might write. Every few weeks Itrò kindly reminded me that I had a small, intelligent readership, and that it would be a pity to allow them to forget about my love for public education.

In brief, things were good with me, I was satisfied with myself like never before, and I coudn't grasp Nadia's apprehension and suspicion. If anything, they grated on my nerves. One time she got mad at Emma in a way that frightened me: she tossed the plate that the child was playing in with her spoon, getting food all over herself, and stormed out of the kitchen, violently slamming the door. Maybe, I thought, maybe she's the one who's unwell. And on that occasion, I thought back to her tormented return from Naples, the tears that had followed, the hostile way she'd barricaded herself behind schoolwork and our daughter. But above all, I realized, that was when she stopped carving out a bit of time to study, and to go down to Naples.

Had the hullabaloo around the book consumed all my attention? Was it possible that I was only realizing this now? I felt the way I did when I was a student, and the professor would catch me when I was distracted. I hated being reprimanded for being distracted, it always felt like a police raid, which is why I never got upset with my students, I didn't press by banging my fists on the podium, or shout at them to pay attention to me. I drew them back to me, to my lecture, with caution, at times even gently. An easily distracted person can always also be easily attracted by something else. When we hooked up, Teresa, who, to be perfectly honest, had been the most distracted student I'd ever had, confessed, in one of her moments of weakness: I started loving you for the kind way that you drew me into your incredibly boring lectures. And I'd replied, so seriously that for days she'd tormented me, sarcastically mocking my voice: I've always felt that call for order was a great shove in the back, which is why I never like to shove people. All this to say that, suddenly, realizing how the business about the book had dimmed Nadia now felt like a rude shock. And almost to justify my lack of attention, I thought: Of course, I'm to blame here, but Nadia has drawn a boundary between the two of us, keeping what happened to her at the university to herself, and no one can say that I didn't insist. If she'd told me the whole story, word for word, it wouldn't have turned out that way. But later, to set things right, one Sunday after lunch, as we were taking in some sun on the balcony, I patiently asked her, once again, why she'd put an end to her studies, why she no longer went to visit her professor.

—You've finally noticed.

—Finally? I noticed right away, but I was being discreet, you told me that was your business.

—And, in fact, it is my business.

—So much so that you can't confide in me?

We spent the night talking about the distinction between her business and my business, until I managed to convince her that my business was also her business, and that it was unfair and maybe even mean of her not to think as I did. She despaired, made an effort to pull herself together, and in the end, confided in me. The penultimate time she'd gone to see the professor, after the usual boring and eternal wait in the corridor that, in spite of having enormous windows, seemed windowless, he, seated as usual behind a massive desk, had greeted her with unusual friendliness. Nadia had spoken to me countless times about that gentleman, always in a positive way. True, she found him surly, and at times cruelly sarcastic toward students both male and female, but he was refined, handsome, highly intelligent, capable now and then even of making a compliment (nice earrings, pretty hair), so much so that I'd say in jest: sure, a handsome old man who courts you, and she'd retort, laughing: better handsome and old than young, dull, and unpleasant. And I would describe him, twisting things— I'd spied him once when I'd gone with her to the university—

as fat, with a gut that hung over his belt, abundant white hair on his bony forehead, eyes that were too blue inside a swollen face, big nose, the line of mouth tight between heavy jowls—and I'd tease her for her excessive devotion. How can you like that old guy when—oh lucky woman that you are—you have me? In any case, she'd gone in, timid, fearful as usual, since the old man was temperamental, and his sunny disposition never lasted long. But his warm welcome had immediately made her go beet red. He'd exclaimed: let's see what lovely thing this young girl has brought me, and Nadia had immediately felt appreciated, she'd pulled out her pages, the little that she'd been able to produce in spite of school, Emma, and me, and standing at the side of the desk, she'd murmured: I haven't made great strides. But she'd immediately regretted playing things down, and she'd blurted out some solution or other, of some significance, handing him the sheets of paper, and he'd seemed interested. Come, he'd said, addressing his informally for the first time, let's go over it together, and he'd made a move with his hand, staring at her in an inviting way, and then he brushed the tips of his fingers against one of his legs. Nadia hadn't quite realized that the old man was asking her to sit on his knees, she was confused, and she drew a little closer to look at her own sheets of paper with him, and the professor had placed his arm around her waist, which was now slumped down a bit, given that she was standing, and he was sitting, and he leaned his torso against her hip as if he'd lost his balance and had to steady himself. Such that Nadia burst out laughing, a nervous laugh. She pulled away, still laughing, and the old man, now laughing in turn, had said where are you going, stay close, don't worry, and she'd sputtered out, still laughing, No Professor, I'm sorry, but I really have to go, and she'd slipped out the door, leaving him behind the desk with her pages in his hand.

My wife said nothing else for a few seconds, and thinking

the story had ended, I said a few things to express my indigna-
tion. But while for Nadia, I immediately realized, that awkward advance by an ancient man was, naturally, a disappoint-
ment—a gifted academic, a famous mathematician, how on
earth could he make himself look so ridiculous, in his own
office, in the very locus of his prestige—she nevertheless
moved past it, and a few days later decided to go back to the
university, for the weakness of the old man didn't matter, what
did was the mighty mathematician's opinion of those pages,
crammed with equations, pages that he'd held onto. That, for
her, had been the really awful part. After the usual eternal wait,
at last the door opened, someone poked out, someone she
knew, an assistant her own age, who'd seen her still there,
who'd smiled at her, gone back in, and then, right then, the
professor could be heard shouting out with a heavy Neapolitan
accent: Good god, that idiot is still here, she never gives up,
please get rid of her.

That was what made me decide—Nadia said quietly. If
there had been something actually worthwhile on those sheets
of paper, he would have pardoned himself for his foolishness,
and since he wasn't one to look away when confronting a flash
of genius, he would have asked me to come in, he would have
praised me, encouraged me. He didn't do that. Instead he
started yelling, and in such an awful way. And so it was clear to
me that I was the one who'd made a mistake, that I'd availed
myself of his attention, his compliments—what a lovely perfume, pretty dress, beautiful earrings—to believe that he
respected me, that I really was smart, whereas I actually have
no talent apart from the small dose of diligence it took to grad-
uate at the top of my class.

That night, and in the days that followed, I went all out to
convince her that what she'd really done was waste her time over
a decrepit old pig. This man's scientific dignity—I told her—
must be pretty scarce if he's grown old in a room reducing

himself to drooling over a beautiful, intelligent woman. It was no use, she got even more depressed: her professor was a world-famous mathematician, I was better off not making pronouncements about things I didn't know about. I told her once:

—You'll see, one of these days we'll read in the papers that he's been arrested, or that an outraged husband like me split his head open with an axe.

—Don't you dare.

—Split his head open with an axe?

—Talk about him that way: if he ends up in trouble, I'll be the first to defend him.

—Seriously?

—Yes.

14.

I felt dark, not in the sense that my spirits darkened, but as if my gaze illuminated Nadia, and left me in the shadows. It went on for a long time; my wife beating herself up while feeling sorry for the old mathematician impoverished by Eros, and I exclaiming that that man must also have a wife, children, grandchildren, admirers—which was why everyone, absolutely everyone should know how loathsomely he'd behaved with one of the most promising mathematicians in Italy. And at that exact time, it was clear how I might see myself in the ancient academic who, I imagined, was afraid that Nadia might spread the word about the foul business he'd conducted. And so, precisely while I was wishing, above all, that the grandchildren knew what a deplorable grandfather they had, I recognized within me, just as sincerely, the fear of humiliation, the shame, and I said to myself: keep quiet, what are you saying, that guy hasn't done anything bad, not compared to what you confided to Teresa, imagine if she came back from America now and talked about it with Nadia, with Tilde, with Itrò, with your readers, and said: you understand the kind of man he is, that Pietro Vella, come on, go get an axe and split his head in two. That's where the darkness originated from, and already, as I was staring at Nadia, talking to her, illuminated by her generous pity, I quickly sought shelter in my dark depression, and softened my words, muttering: rushing to save a filthy old pig who's ruining your career seems truly excessive to me; but maybe I'm being too hard on him, I didn't mean the stuff about the axe and splitting his head in two.

From that moment, slowly, the terrible things my wife had gone through became a joke between us. If, in the course of opening a particularly stubborn can of beans, I summoned the axe I wanted to use for the Fucking Academic God—that was now my name for the old mathematician—we'd burst out laughing. And in the beginning I laughed a lot, she less, and then it was her turn to laugh a lot while I piped down. After a bit I convinced myself that the worst was over, and one Sunday afternoon we got into bed, when Emma was at her grandparents', and she pressed up against me whispering, Come inside me, it's the right time. I understood what she was implying, and I happily obeyed. A month later she was pregnant, she was excited to carry the child, and then Sergio was born.

But Nadia wasn't satisfied. During her second pregnancy, she started to study English and Spanish, she struggled to read novels in their original languages, and she wanted nothing more to do with algebraic surfaces. Given that she now spoke to me mixing bits of foreign languages into her Italian, she started up a little ditty about how lovely it was to be *incinta*, pregnant, *embarazada*. One night she murmured into my ear, laughing nervously, forget the condom, embarrass me a third time, impregnate me. I was disoriented. I asked: are you joking or being serious? She wasn't joking. At the very same time that

women, even those in Valle Peligna, were trying to overthrow
their suffocating lives, Nadia had decided to overwhelm herself with math homework, me, and lots of kids. And so I made
her happy, and I did this, above all, because it seemed that
being pregnant suffused her with an engaging vitality. But the
third time around was so tough, the labor so complicated, and
life with three small children so hard—the last one, Ernesto,
was born enormous but then immediately turned thin and
inconsolable—that she no longer turned to books, she stopped
studying foreign languages, and now she only asked: did you
check, are you sure the condom didn't break?

15.

In those years, I published several articles in scholastic magazines both large and small, as well as—though less frequently—in prominent national newspapers, and they were all
positively received. Since I was increasingly astonished by my
success, I began to ask myself why I continued to be astonished, given that Tilde, Itrò, Nadia, and by now a reasonably
sized audience were no longer in the least bit astonished. I told
myself that it was based on the fact that, until I was thirty years
old, nothing had ever happened to me that would have proven,
to me first of all, that I was superior to most of my peers. From
the very start of elementary school, I'd proven to be an utterly
average student. At university, no professor ever took note of
me, and I'd graduated with middling grades. I'd received my
teacher's certificate in a conspicuously high number of subjects
and had passed a deadly dull examination to finally be
assigned a post, but in both cases I had never received especially high grades. Yes, I was regarded, for years, as a good
teacher, but mostly because I knew that I knew quite little, so
I studied diligently each day, I was prompt in correcting home-

work, and I was always prepared and cheerful in class. In brief, nothing had happened in my life that would allow me to attenuate that congenital dissatisfaction I had with myself. And besides, even now that things kept getting better, even though I was happy that my articles were being met with enthusiasm, if I compared myself to Tilde, to Professor Itrò, to Nadia, and let's not even mention Teresa, I told myself: what am I compared to them? A simple brain with a superficial smattering of learning, a newly acculturated being without solid traditions, excessive in my ways, in my propositions, in the way I spoke, lacking the refinement one possesses only when it is passed down from one cultured generation to the next. Tilde, now she's extraordinary: so learned, she speaks four languages, she's travelled, ranks of cultured ancestors have gone into making her who she is. And Itrò, what an extraordinary man, when he talks about education, he really knows what he's saying. And Nadia, the daughter of a school principal and a teacher, top of her class with highest honors in math, a highly intelligent woman, she really did deserve the academic career she'd always dreamed of. And Teresa, now there's a brain. I met her when she was sixteen, the daughter of a humble family who nevertheless sparkled from the minute she was born. She sat at the back, at the desk beside the window, and if you take away all her flaws, all her unruly behavior, she was always a hundred times ahead compared to the other students, as opposed to anyone I've ever met, maybe even compared to Tilde, to Itrò, to Nadia, without of course dragging myself into it. And so, when I turned these thoughts over and over in my head, and perceived, even more acutely, the schism between the public image that I was slowly acquiring and the way I really felt—a teacher from the outskirts, a struggling head of the family, a distracted husband who, when cornered, pretended not to be, rather, not to have ever been distracted—I started to write a new book in which I further developed the idea that public schools had never functioned as they should have; that the biggest hypocrisy was to distribute equal portions of knowledge to those who were unequal, pretending that they were equals; which meant that quality teaching for all meant, in fact, upending not just the classroom, but also the family, society, the hierarchy of knowledge, religion, the ownership of the means of production, all of it; that the failure, by now evident, of public education for the masses would cause more irreversible damage than a nuclear war. The school system, I hoped to conclude, had to be reconceived so as to provide everyone, absolutely everyone, and above all teachers, the means to envision their greatness and, at the ideal moment, to wake up and achieve it.

I made time to write between teaching, Nadia's pregnancies, and long meetings with Tilde and Itrò, who had taken it upon themselves to make sure I didn't fritter away my hours. In that long span of time, especially when Nadia was pregnant with Sergio and was exceptionally radiant, Tilde and Professor Itrò often came to dinner at our place, with their spouses, and they got to know Emma, and they befriended my wife. Sometimes we'd take them on a walk through the quiet streets of our neighborhood, to see a garden, or to admire a tree, or to drink from a fountain that contained mineral water. Naturally they were delighted: what a lovely breeze, so fragrant, we ate so well, delicious cake. But then Itrò always ended up saying: as soon as you say the word, I'll find a way to transfer you to a high school in the center of the city; and then he'd say to Nadia, with the good manners of a refined gentleman: Nadia, I understand, it's a family house, but you're a remarkable woman, never mind your husband, and the two of you should get yourselves an apartment that's more central.

My wife shook her head. She was grateful to Itrò for the frequent compliments he paid to her intelligence, but she got slightly annoyed when he set in on Emma's future: what would you like to do with this marvelous young lady, she deserves the best, and not only the magnificent Abruzzo of her grandparents, lucky girl. Nadia didn't argue, Itrò was Itrò, he was bursting with superiority; but she remained pensive for a few days, and out of the blue, taking for granted that I could read her thoughts even though she'd never organized them out loud, she blurted out things like: if I hadn't been born in Pratola Peligna, if I'd grown up in the center of Rome, do you think I'd be teaching at a university by now? I'd counter: oh, come on, that's not what Itrò meant, Pratola Peligna is a great place, Montesacro isn't a dump, it's just a fixation of his, he's always lived in the center and he wants us nearby, wants us to teach and live nearby, because he admires us, and he'd like to see us more often.

One time, however, when she was pregnant with Ernesto and unwell, and I wanted to prevent her from spiraling yet again, and bashing herself over her inadequacies, whether real or presumed, I committed a grave error. As usual she complained: maybe I screwed everything up, maybe we really should be giving our kids every opportunity, and she felt guilty for the way we were raising Emma and Sergio. I said: what are you talking about, look at Teresa, you remember her, she was born and raised on the outskirts, her parents ran a little bar that was always on the verge of shutting down, unlearned people, she even had me as her literature teacher, poor girl; but now she works at MIT.

—Teresa your ex?

—Ex, please, that was ages ago, I don't even remember what she was like anymore.

She shouted:

—Get the hell out of here, go back to her, go to America. You're so smart, I'm sure you'll do great things there, too.

Of course, everything blows over, and so she seemed to forget my inopportune words. Meanwhile, for the launch of my new book, Tilde organized an interview with an important weekly magazine. Until then, I'd never done anything of the kind. Only a few words on the phone, that then turned into two lines in an article that included the opinions of ten other people much more relevant than I was. Instead, on that occasion, in the publisher's Rome offices, a quite prominent journalist at the time (how quickly one's notoriety fades) came just for me, and he asked me a boatload of questions and let me talk for an hour and a half. Then he exchanged a few words with Tilde and left. She approached me, radiant. She hugged me, kissed me a centimeter from my lips, and said:

—You've won him over.

—It's not true.

—It is: you have no idea of the effect you have when you start talking.

—It's just by rote: I've given lessons all day, for years.

—No, no, and no. I need to take better care of you, I need to teach you what you are. Your problem is that you don't know it.

—I know perfectly well: I'm the product of a lousy postwar education—the schools were still fascist, and only of late, falsely republican—that afflicted an enormous number of kids who needed teachers to do a decent job.

—Oh stop, the interview's finished.

—When will it come out?

—I don't know. Before the presentation in Milan, I hope.

There was still time before Milan. I was overwhelmed by the end of the school year and final exams, and so the interview slipped from my mind. In the meantime, the book appeared in bookstores. I was suddenly worried that I'd written it too quickly, and that all my fans would realize they'd made a big mistake, and that some big-name scholar would be so indignant that he'd write: whatever happened to the lovely Italian of the past, the long, elaborate arguments, the cultured reasoning? Our schools have fallen into the hands of people like these, etcetera, etcetera.

One afternoon I came back home, exhausted. Nadia's belly
was huge, she was about to give birth, and she was screaming
at Sergio as if he were an adult as opposed to a cheerful two-
year-old. I said:

—Take a break, I'll take over now, you look beat.

—And what the fuck do you care if I'm beat?

She never talked like this. I got scared, and said quietly:

—Go on, lie down for a bit.

—You go lie down. You worked, you've earned it.
Meanwhile go read *Panorama* in peace.

She pointed to the kitchen at the end of the hallway. Emma
was at the table, kneeling on a chair. I joined her. She was leaf-
ing through a magazine—no wait—she was looking at no less
than a picture of me, boxed in the middle of the page. I held
back my worry, my impatience.

—How did it turn out? I asked Nadia who, at the other end
of the hallway, had started yelling at Sergio again, with an
anger that she surely would have liked to shower over me. She
announced gloomily:

—It's stunning.

—Really?

—Would I lie? It goes on for two pages.

Her tone was unbearable. I thought she was complaining
because, as usual, she had to run the household, and teach, and
deal with two children, and a third that was still lodged for a
short while in her belly. I said, kindly:

—I'll read it later. Sergio, come to Papà.

—I want you to read it right now.

—Nadia, don't get upset.

—You think I'm upset? Emma, give Papà the magazine.

Emma was incredibly proud of my picture. First she kissed
me all over, then she wanted to kiss the page. I finally managed
to wrest the magazine away from her, but only as long as she
could sit on my knees as I read. A nice title. If memory serves

me well, it spoke of resurrection. My book—I read in the sum-
mary—restored life to the debate over an institution everyone
said they cared about, but no one paid attention to. And in the
generous introduction, the plaudits were over the top, there
were even a few brief quotes, things I'd written, so incisive that
I couldn't believe I'd even written them. As for the actual
interview, the journalist had managed to make my replies
sound interesting and always elegant.

I was thrilled and pleased with myself. I never thought that
an hour and a half of meandering conversation could result in an
article as acutely intelligent as this. I no longer heard Nadia, who
was bickering with Sergio about something, and I only remembered her when I sensed her standing in the kitchen doorway. I
looked up, and in that brief instant, I thought she looked ill. She
had a greenish pallor, her ankles were swollen, her enormous
belly barely contained by a dress that bunched up at the sides
because our son clung to it, seeking affection. I thought: why is
she so dissatisfied, I'm her husband, the father of her children,
she should be happy about the impression I make: the better
things go for me, the better off her life, and Emma's, and
Sergio's, and that of the baby who's about to arrive.

—Well—she stared at me, her eyes distraught.

—Sit down, come here, tell me how you're doing.

—Did you read it?

—I did, it's nice.

—Are you satisfied with yourself?

—A little.

—And did you turn the page? Did you see the wonderful
company you're in?

I didn't know what she was saying, I asked, what page? But
meanwhile, Emma had already done what her mother was asking, and I saw that, right after my interview, there was another
one, with a picture bigger than mine. I recognized Teresa right
away, just as Nadia was saying, commandingly: Emma, come to

Mamma, Papà's busy. And she said this with such anger, so poorly concealed, that the girl quickly slid off my knees and ran behind her mother and her brother, as if all three of them were running from an earthquake, or rather, the four of them.

16.

A few days later Nadia gave birth to Ernesto, our third child. The birth—I've already mentioned—was as hard as the pregnancy had been. I cancelled all my appointments and forced myself, above all, to forget that at the end of the interview, it said that Teresa would be speaking about something or other in Rome, at the university, in exactly nine days from then, at ten in the morning. I now knew perfectly well that my wife thought that I was dying to run to see her, which was why, before her water broke, I did all I could to reassure her. After giving birth she was in such bad shape that I don't think either of us paid heed to that conference. Even though a small part of me suspected, now and again, that all the pain of giving birth to Ernesto had been staged by her body to remind me how much the thought of my going to hear Teresa's brilliant talk weighed on her.

Naturally, there was no way to explain to her that I was afraid to see my former student and lover, just as there was no way to explain that, precisely because I was afraid of Teresa in that very moment, I was desperate to see her, talk to her, calm myself down. So, I proceeded to run through all the plausible lies I could muster, but couldn't manage to settle on one. The clinic discharged Nadia and the baby the very same day as the conference at the university. I had to tend to my wife and child, take them home, assume my paternal responsibilities. Though assisted by an incredibly capable mother-in-law who came down from Pratola for the occasion, I had to be on call at every moment, given that my companion was a wreck, and my first two children didn't like the third, who wasn't cute, and unwillingly accepted the task of living.

To complicate things further, the sense of irritation I had toward myself reemerged in that period. I didn't enjoy dedicating myself to Nadia and my three children, all the while turning myself inside out over the fact that I was missing the chance to see Teresa, and reinforcing our relationship to feel safer. It was a torment, but I rose to the task. Exactly when she was surely in Rome, and I might have attempted to track her down, I took it upon myself to take care of Nadia with all the love I could muster, to the degree that my wife appeared to settle down, and the following week, it was she who insisted that I shouldn't skip my book launch in Milan. Obviously, I sensed that she was making a huge effort, that she wanted me at home, and it upset me to see her suffer. Her body suffered, and she suffered thinking of the thousand ways she'd given up, of ways she'd failed and things she'd lost. She suffered for the three children who, after wanting to have them, after practically having ordered me to have them, she now suddenly felt were a weight, a weight in the literal sense of the weight of heavy objects: wardrobes, boulders, entire skyscrapers. She said, more than once: I'm so sad I can't go with you. She declared, regretfully: I'm sure Tilde bought herself something fantastic to wear. She murmured: I wish so much I could hear her talk about your book, she always has such meaningful things to say. And she even went so far as to point out the dress and the shoes she would have worn for the occasion. Instead, limping, in disarray, she packed my suitcase. I left with a sense of freedom.

17.

I found Tilde in her powerful car, which she drove up to

Milan. Goodness she loved to drive, she did so effortlessly, and we only stopped two or three times for gas, a bite to eat, and trips to the bathroom. The rest of the time we were thick in conversation, as we always were on those occasions, in the car, at dinner, in hotels.

We talked about everything, and she had amazing insights on each topic—fleet, elegant, and incredibly numerous—drawn out with such panache, that at a certain point they felt excessive, and sounded like truisms. In the recent past, we'd also been talking about sex, a subject she relished and always spoke about cheerfully. On and on she went, hiding nothing from me by now. Sometimes we kept talking after dinner, we'd drink an herbal tea, then have some hard liquor, and keep bantering, repairing to our rooms only at the crack of dawn.

That was how things went the first night in Milan. We got there around ten at night, and I called home to make sure nothing awful had happened. I felt better, and I ran straightaway with Tilde to the restaurant just steps from the hotel. Not satisfied with having talked nonstop during the journey, we kept talking, laughing, joking with one another. Before we withdrew to our rooms I observed:

—By now I know more about your body, what you like in bed, and your idiosyncrasies than I would if we'd been sleeping together for the past five years.

She replied:

—There's always more to learn.

—If one wants to, sure, I admitted, and said goodnight. I returned, worn out, to my room. After a few minutes she knocked and asked, soberly:

—But do you want to?

—What.

—Learn more.

—Yes.

—Now?

I was about to say, OK, but then I thought of the children sleeping in their little beds, and Nadia who'd surely not slept all night, and tiny, ugly Ernesto. I said:

—You're tired, you've driven up from Rome. Better tomorrow.

—Yes, you're right. Get some rest.

But I couldn't sleep. I hadn't ever betrayed Nadia until then; it had never even occurred to me that I could. Of course, in that phase of pleasant personal growth, I'd felt, on more than one occasion, respected, admired. In Tilde's case there had just been greater continuity, and naturally I'd thought that if, gradually, I'd forced the rules of the game, our taste for those seductive expressions would lead in all likelihood to coitus, and the imaginative workings of bodies pushed to their limits. And yet I never felt the urge to do it, I was too enamored of the idea of myself that I was building, and I didn't want to ruin it with embarrassing equivocations, useless contrivances, and the minor, casual pleasures that belonged to the unsatisfying life I'd once had, back when I'd cheat on Teresa whenever I could, with girls I didn't even like. When she no doubt cheated on me with whoever expressed interest in her. But with Tilde things were already too advanced, in every sense. Above all, she struck me as a woman so superior to me that, from minute to minute, a part of me felt that she was utterly in sync with my currently unfolding life, a sort of blazing fulfilment of the person I was becoming, my friend, my advisor, my instructor, and therefore, why not, my lover.

I woke up early in the morning as if I'd made love to her all night, exhausted and maybe also a bit depressed. We had the usual pleasant breakfast together, even though she, in spite of her skillful makeup, had signs of weariness in her face and a troubled look in her eyes. I went back to my room and called Nadia, who reassured me that she was feeling fine, as were Ernesto and Emma and Sergio, and that her mother was still attentively present. After that, I turned up in the lobby again, and we went to a school where three hundred students and nearly a dozen teachers awaited me in their auditorium.

It was an enjoyable morning. I talked about the book, and I navigated replies to scores of intelligent questions. And from the presentation on, I didn't have a break. Tilde had organized a lunch right afterwards with a renowned professor from the Cattolica and with the local council member in charge of education, culture, and sports. It was exhausting, and I was afraid of revealing huge gaps, of appearing misinformed, of having flimsy things to say. But Tilde was savvy at public relations, and it all went smoothly. Right after that, we hopped into a taxi that catapulted us to the home of an elderly lady, a princess, as Tilde happily explained. I didn't tell her that I didn't understand, nearly two hundred years after the French Revolution, why people spoke with admiration and devotion of princes and princesses. I just focused on the task at hand: to make a good impression on the noblewoman, something which, according to Tilde, would come naturally to me. And so it did. The old blueblood was nearly ninety years old, but she was sharp as a whip, and funny. She'd read my first book and quickly read the second. She'd been and still was among the finest connoisseurs of the life and works of Maria Montessori. We spoke for over two hours, nibbling on pastries and drinking black tea in an environment the likes of which—with its carpets, furnishings, paintings on the walls, and stuccos—I'd only seen in films. She mentioned a staggering number of famous people, both dead and living, calling them by name rather than surname. Tilde helped me to solve the rebus of figuring out who they were by providing speedy prompts, and the noble lady gossiped about all of them, delighting in telling me about their turpitudes, financial blemishes, sexual perversions, and cruelty combined with their ignorance and superficiality.

She's never talked at such length to anyone, Tilde exclaimed when we finally left the apartment. She usually calls it a day after five minutes: You have a gift, you do, you put people at ease. Her satisfaction, and the pride with which she spoke of me, transmitted a sense of power that immediately transformed into a desire to hold her tight, pull her toward me, and fuck her. No, she said prudently, and merely interlaced her fingers with mine in the elevator, letting go as soon as we stepped out. Thus galvanized, we arrived slightly late in a bookstore, where I had to talk about my new book. And what if no one shows up, I asked, suddenly seized by my old anxiety. Tilde laughed, took a quick look round, and pinched my thigh: if there's no one, she said, her eyes twinkling, oh well, it's a lovely evening, the weather's mild, we'll take a walk; but you'll see, a few people will turn up.

In fact, the room was overflowing, and I was thrilled to be there, to have a woman like her at my side, to finally be me, to be the me I wanted to be, the me that my father and all my serf ancestors must have dreamed of, the me who'd written two books, the me who was the pensive author able to draw scores of highbrow people out of their homes and out of their busy schedules, people willing to discuss, at least for an hour, a traditionally boring topic.

The owner of the bookstore talked first, then Tilde, in her typically quick and persuasive way, chimed in, and finally it was my turn. I stood up. I never felt I had a good grip on the audience if I was sitting down, even when I taught, I never sat behind the desk. I cleared my throat and, a second before I began to utter words, Teresa appeared at the back of the room. It was what I feared most. There she was, there was no escape, wherever I went, she'd find a way to remind me of who I am. And not when I want her to, but whenever she wants. And as usual, she'll say whatever she feels like, like the ninety-year-old princess, even though she's young and doesn't have a drop of blue blood in her.

Now that she stood before me after several years, I worked harder than usual. I aimed to get her to listen the way I would when I was her teacher, and she sat at the back of the room, beside the window, and was an unruly girl. The whole time, I was ostensibly speaking to the audience, but I was really talking to her. I set in with all I had to give, all my skills, in order to convince her that now I'd been purified, and that I deserved all the respect that she probably hadn't handed me when I'd been her teacher, when I'd been her lover. I talked for nearly an hour; I didn't want to stop. I trained my eyes on her, and since I didn't pick up on any sign of acknowledgement, not even the shadow of a smile, I said to myself: I have to talk longer, I have to somehow overcome that hostility of hers, I have to rouse her, make her laugh, in other words, loosen her up the way I once knew how. But it was useless, not once did I sense that agreeable yielding that, by now, I'd learned to recognize in public, even with total strangers, people with whom I'd never exchange another word. Teresa never moved, she remained in a tight frame between the heads of other people who hadn't found a seat, and I felt her piercing gaze fixed on me, on the verge of rendering itself as a sarcastic comment. It was time for me to wrap up, and for the owner of the bookstore to ask the audience if they had questions. Teresa probably would have been the first to ask one; she was never one to feel intimidated, and who knew what she'd say? Derisive things, some denigrating account of what kind of teacher I'd been. Oh god, best not to think of it. I kept going until Tilde gestured with her hand to signal: stop, and so I stopped, and I sat down, wiped out, while a burst of applause rang out.

—Who is she? she asked in my ear.

—Who?

—You know who, the woman at the back to the right. You only talked to her, for an hour.

—That's not true.

—Yes it is.

18.

The Q&A began. At first no one wanted to intervene, and they looked awkwardly at the floor; every audience resembles a group of schoolchildren. Then an old teacher in the first row started talking, and then many more people started making comments. I always gave sober replies, and at a certain point, even cheerful ones given that, contrary to my expectations, Teresa gave no sign of wanting to speak and, rather, seemed to be hiding. From where I was seated, all I could see was the jocund mass of her jet-black hair.

The owner of the bookstore intervened after a solid half-hour to say there was time for just one more question. I stared at the table, nervous, and I heard a woman's voice ask me what I thought of my scholastic journey. It wasn't Teresa, but an impeccably trained student, probably the best in her class in one of the city's finest high schools. My glasses were perched on my forehead. They slid down my nose. Danger averted.

—Terrible, I said, keeping my eye on Teresa, who was now visible again at the back of the room.

—Don't you think that one who speaks ill of his school loses credibility, as if you're saying: I don't have the right training to be in this position, to play the Cabinet member, to write books or speak in public?

I replied:

—Yes, and I then wanted to explain myself thoroughly, list the consequences. But a second after I said Yes, I saw-heard

Teresa, who was clapping her hands loudly, and since one pair of clapping hands unleashes the applause of many, everyone, even the student who had asked the question, applauded me at length, excited, as if they felt, in that moment, that their schooling had been terrible and were happy to declare so with their applause.

The evening had reached its conclusion, and many people were heading out. I searched for Teresa among those who lingered, among those who already thronged the table to ask me to sign my book. I didn't see her, as I was in the grip of my readers. A few, who hadn't asked questions but had them ready on the tips of their tongues, wanted to ask them now, one on one. A pair of elegant women, perhaps twins, recited a list of all those who, in spite of not having gone to school or having done poorly, had gone on to do great things in the sciences and the arts. I continued to fend for myself, speaking jovially, until Tilde took me by the arm, thanked all those who still lingered, and dragged me away, whispering into my ear: no formal dinner tonight, it's just you and me, but first I need to work out a few issues with the bookstore. You head back to the hotel, we'll eat something there.

The hotel was close by. I drank in the air of a summer's evening in Milan, my temples were throbbing, and I felt hot. I examined the street furtively, looking sidelong at the pedestrians, at the clusters of teachers who were still hanging around. I was glad that Teresa had left, and at the same time this upset me. The contradiction got on my nerves, but meanwhile, that's how things really were: I didn't feel like talking to her, and yet I believed it necessary: if she'd gone back to America, which was, moreover, what the interview had said, who knew when we would be able to speak alone. And speaking to say what: when we write, we can calibrate our words; whereas, in face-to-face conversations, we risk saying too much, and reawaken what's dormant. I'll write her another letter, I thought to myself, it's better that way. But just as I was calming down, assigning myself the task, I saw her on the corner, in front of a café, with two or three friends, or people she'd just met, all of them men.

I'll call out to her, I resolved, but then I immediately changed my mind. She would have dismissed me with some ironic quip about my lecture, which would have been intended to get a laugh out of her group of courtiers or co-workers whom she'd forcibly dragged to listen to my trivial remarks. Maybe they were also scientists, Americans, or of some other origin. Teresa knew lots of languages, certainly compared to my Latin, Ancient Greek, and Neapolitan. She was remarkably at ease; I could tell just from looking. Thin build, jeans and a little blouse, young, unleashed. Looking at her, I was already reassessing my meagre successes in recent years. I was a man who lacked the vision trained to see past the puddle of Italy, one that was stuck in the gutters of the Roman outskirts. She, on the other hand, there she was, on the other side of the street, a polyglot scientist of international renown, the student who had surpassed her teacher, teacher meanwhile of what, I didn't know a thing about the subjects she shone in. I shouted: ciao, Teresa, and I moved on, with long strides, my head lowered, my right arm raised and weakly waving to say goodbye.

But after only a few minutes I heard a shuffling of feet, and I'd hardly had the time to turn around before she linked her arm with mine.

—Where are you going? Do you have a date with that good-looking gal who monitors every word you say?

—I didn't want to interrupt.

—Oh, but I did.

She set in right away, making fun of my speech—such fire, such fervor! Too much. From where I was standing, you looked like a big animal doing tricks for its owner—and then she pushed me into a café, and when she pulled her arm away,

I felt the fabric of my jacket quickly cooling off; I was already losing that heat she'd passed on to me. All of us, I countered, laughing, are big old animals when it comes right down to it. And meanwhile I was glancing regretfully at my watch: sorry, Teresa, I only have two minutes to spare, I'm off to something else. She pretended not to hear me, picked out a table, sat down, and began to quote my letters back to me—the news I'd given her about Nadia, about the children—but it was as if I'd lied to her, and she had to work to eke out the truth between the lines. I looked at my watch again, I nodded to the barista, but she was already telling me sarcastically what she'd deduced from my words: Nadia was my servant, the victim on whom I inflicted cruelty while pretending to be attentive to her, the woman whose marrow I sucked in order to fortify myself and go out on the road playing the part of the brilliant man with women who were enemies to other women; as for the children, in her eyes they must have been scrawny things, obligated to be loving because of the terror I instilled in them. I was practically a stranger to them, even when I went home I wasn't there, all I thought about were my own affairs, an unaffectionate gorilla, always on the hunt, who dreamed of prey even when he wasn't hunting. You haven't changed a bit, I said, resorting to an amused tone of voice similar to hers. You delight in deconstructing the lives of others, mine above all. And she exclaimed, feigning remorse: see, I've offended you, obviously I was kidding, you were fantastic in the bookstore, you're the best of men, a good husband, an excellent father, I was only quoting a lecture you gave when I was in my penultimate year of high school. She wanted to synthesize it for me. I was so shaken by it, she said. You teachers should measure each word instead of drowning us in a sea of discourse. I'd said: there's nothing human that can't be traced back to a growl, an argh, an ugh, an ooh ooh ooh: all of it, even poetry, even the broken gates of dawn, even the suns that strike the eyelashes, was composed of growls. And here she made a gesture with her finger, which was most likely a parody of one of my teaching gestures, and then concluded: see how I still remember every word you said?

Yes, it was true, she remembered something. She'd surprised me by quoting Zanzotto; I was the one who had made her read him when I was her teacher. They were words I loved, still quoted to my senior-year students, and I felt a flicker of pride for the fact that she'd retained them in her memory. I was therefore an indelible part of her education, and it flattered me to have contributed in earnest to create the person she was. I softened my stance. I told her I wasn't in the least bit offended, that I was happy to be a gorilla, that I was in a phase when the growls— argh, ugh, ooh ooh ooh—came quite naturally, and that, on the other hand, I really did have very little time, an appointment was an appointment, I can't afford to look disrespectful.

That firm tone turned her immediately chilly, and her eyes grew still. Go on then, I'm fine, you're fine, go give even more seductive speeches than before, you have a family more functional than the holy family, we've both become so interesting that they put us in the papers, goodbye then, kisses. Then she made a sign as if to get up, and though I knew she was faking it, I quickly grabbed her wrist to hold her back. I smiled at her and said softly, two minutes are two minutes, let's let them pass. And I ordered two beers, knowing that she liked to drink beer. I ordered her favorite one. She stayed seated, and said, soberly, in a way she almost never did:

—Do you want to waste the little time you've got, or should we get straight to the point?

—What's the point?

—The point is that if you still remember me, if you write me long letters (how are you, what's America like, how do you get by, do you have a boyfriend, a husband, are you a mother, what's your job?), it's for a reason that you don't have the courage to say clearly.

—There's only one reason, and it's quite clear: I'm fond of you.

—No, the reason is that you want to know if I am, and will always be, the faithful custodian of what you confided in me.

I shook my head vigorously.

—I've never not trusted you.

—Liar.

—It's true. At most, I worry that you might get distracted at some point. We've both entered into a pleasant phase of life, and I'd hate it if, due to some foolishness, some surge, some stupid joke, we ended up hurting each other.

—See how worried you are?

I shook my head again, behaving like a person who feels misunderstood. And at that point, Teresa made a move that, in all the years of our relationship, was unheard of, a gesture of gratuitous affection: she extended her arm and brushed her pale finger on the back of my hand. She then admitted that, in our own way, with some lack of moderation that was also cruel, we had loved each other deeply. She said: now that some years have gone by, I'm well aware of it. And sometimes, when I feel alone, on the other side of the world, I even end thinking that we still love each other; sure, living together didn't work out. Rather, I suspect that the effort of living together had soured our natures back then, and that we would turn even worse were we to be together again. But by remaining separate, we can be a solid couple.

—A couple? You and me?

She drank the last of her beer, then she fixed her sardonic eyes on mine.

—Of course: I'll watch over you forever, and you over me.

—What do you mean?

—We'll get married. We'll have a kind of wedding that's not religious, or even a civil ceremony, but, how should we define it? Ethical. If one of us gets out of line, the other has the right to say to anyone at all: now I'll tell you who that man really is, who that woman really is.

I looked at her, perplexed. Was she joking, or being serious? She was proposing a form of control from afar, a hyper-exacting superego who, for the next fifty years, would speak to me with her voice, and to her with mine? What an imaginative girl, too bad I couldn't handle her for more than an hour at a time. Her brain bore through everything, she shone in science and in literature, and she bore a need for an intense life, she was a steel wire that vibrated against the skin, cutting it. Such courage, such guts: these days, this is how most girls tend to be, but not back then. Teresa had been a piece of the future that had shot out of the Roman outskirts. Farewell parents, farewell friends and relatives, farewell to the mountain rising and falling, farewell, above all, to me. She'd left Italy, she'd hopped on planes I'd never set foot on, she'd entered into a world and customs and languages I didn't have a clue about, she'd faced challenges of all kinds, been obstructed by men and women of pedestrian, all-too-common malice, and nevertheless she'd never let up, she'd gotten better and better, she'd boiled it all down to just herself.

I didn't reply. I just gave a nearly silent little laugh and let her embellish the proposal of marriage she'd just made. Now she spoke in a way that was more familiar to me, every sentence poised between seduction and derisive lashings, a voice that was ironic but lacking indulgence, always on the edge of sarcasm. The two minutes expanded, and I was beginning to enjoy being in the café with her on my second beer. Tilde slipped from my mind, as did the evening call to my wife and children. Teresa started to goad me, all she needed was a quick glance from the back of the room to figure out what had, by now, developed between me and Tilde, and what was about to happen that evening. That was some dress Madam Drop-dead was wearing, she said. Do you realize how much time that exquisite queen spends at the mirror doing her makeup, exercising, maintaining herself with creams that you need to rob a bank to buy for yourself? She spends more money in a day than I'll save up in my whole life. But I get it, women like that, they have style. Under that dress you'll find the most sumptuous lingerie, fumes of delicate perfume, not a lick of fat on her abdomen, zero cellulite, and limbs agile enough to satisfy your wildest fantasies. But watch out. Fucking her is a bad move. If you run off to hop into bed with her now, you'll humiliate your wife. And you have two choices. The first: go home, talk to poor Nadia, say the usual things: I was overcome with desire, I'm so sorry, it won't happen again. You'll say this to her in a heartfelt, penitent way, you'll deploy your much touted verbal elegance, you'll fashion your gorilla grunts into lovely well-cadenced sentences. Ooh ooh ooh.

I cut in, speaking like someone who decides, just for the fun of it, to stay in the game.

—Out of the question. Nadia would kick me out of the house, and I'd never see my kids again.

—And so?

—So, I'm not telling her anything. And if things turn complicated, I'll lie. What's the second possibility?

—The second possibility is that I, somehow, come to learn that you've cheated on your wife.

—Ah, and so?

—So I, in my role as your ethical consort, feel betrayed, and I tell whomever I want the worst things about you.

—You mean to say that I either confess everything to my wife, or I give up that woman?

—Yes.

I laughed, this time with nervous over-the-top delight.

—Ok, I'll give her up.

Teresa went back to caressing my hand.

—Bravo. If you keep behaving like this you'll become the best of the best.

—You too, given that, the first time you mess up, you risk the exact same thing I risk.

—I'm fine, I'm already well-behaved.

We said goodbye around eleven o'clock, like two old war buddies who meet up again after their experiences on many battlefields and, by telling each other tales of the barracks, exorcize their dreadful past.

19.

I headed toward the hotel, walking quickly, hands in my pockets. It was almost eleven o'clock; it would be tough explaining myself to Tilde. But I doubted she was asleep, and I desired her, I'd desired her all day, even though it was hard to tell if it was an autonomous desire on my part, or one derived from the certainty that she desired me and was waiting for me. Teresa's playful threats hadn't changed my mind. Desiring a woman even if you're married isn't evil. Teresa had simply jousted a bit with her words: she'd used petty adultery, about to be fulfilled after years of fidelity, as a foil, just to make conversation. At the end of it all, what did she mean to suggest? She meant to suggest that, because of the things we'd confessed to each other, both she and I tended to think that the other was base. But the turn that our lives had taken indicated exactly the opposite: in this terrible world we lived in, we were good people. Only that, unlike the other good people, we knew we could also become base, we knew it so well that due to innate honesty, we had put ourselves in the base category, and now believed that our goodness was a fiction. Instead, we didn't pretend at all, we really were good—good people who now and then did awful things. This was because life was terrible, and whoever was exposed to it ran a continuous risk. But Good Lord, the harm that we good people could commit was never serious compared to what base people were capable of doing. Sure, evil is evil. And yet, wasn't even thinking of a proposition of this kind—evil is evil, without qualifications—proof that we circulated in a system of goodness? One had to aspire to cold, inflexible perfection in order to feel base the minute one stepped out of line. But becoming an adult—I told myself—means giving up, in fact, on perfection. Therefore, yes, ethical marriage, lovely and affectionate conversation, it's a nice game. I, however, now wanted, at all costs, to conclude the evening by slowly taking off Tilde's intimate apparel. I could already feel them under my hands: the tepid, slightly humid fabrics, clothes just pressed by an iron, poker-hot.

I stepped into the hotel, out of breath. She was in the lobby, sitting with her legs crossed on a gilt-framed armchair, and reading some of the page-proofs she always carried around with her.

—Your wife called twice, she said. Since they told her you weren't in the hotel, the third time she called, she asked for me.

—Sorry, I was held up.

—No need to explain yourself to me, but to her yes. I told her that the event went long and that it dragged on even after the bookstore closed.

—I'll give her a call.

—I'll wait for you.

—Did you have dinner?

—An hour ago. You?

—I didn't eat.

—Shall I order you a sandwich?

—Thanks.

I ran off to call Nadia. She picked up with the voice she had when, for some reason or other, I would wake her up.

—Why are you calling me? What time is it?

—Ten past eleven.

—You know I'm asleep at this hour.

—I wanted to tell you that it all went well.

—I know, I spoke with Tilde. What made you so late?

—There were teachers who wanted to keep talking, and they dragged me to a café that was close to the bookstore.

—You tired?

—A little.

—Go to bed.

—The kids?

—They're fine.

—Good night.

—Good night.

I went back to Tilde, relieved. Nadia had sounded calm. I devoured the sandwich, drank another beer, spoke jokingly with her, and she spoke jokingly with me.

—Done?

—Yes.

We left the gilt-framed armchairs and headed toward the elevator, now talking about the proofs Tilde was reading. She pressed the button for the fourth floor. My room was on three. We kept talking about the proofs as if it were the only subject that really mattered to us. She stepped out of the elevator and I followed her. She searched for her key, and I kept suggesting random ways to improve the text in the event that she wanted to publish it. She opened the door to her room, stepped inside, and I stepped in after her, leaving the door open. She turned around, placed her bag on a chair, and asked:

—Aren't you going to close the door?

I distinctly recall the very long beat that followed that question. I suddenly sensed that I had no real need to embrace that woman, to caress her, to enter her body in multiple ways in spite of the exhausting day and my drooping eyelids. I closed the door, and she said:

—I need to go to the bathroom.

She disappeared from the room with a graceful step, almost

on tiptoes. I was alone. I looked around the room that was identical to the one I had on the third floor. I heard water running. The desire remained, yes, but not the necessity: nothing and no one was commanding me to extract pleasure from Tilde's body and sleep with her in that room. It was merely a matter of deciding: either to snip the threads that, almost unawares, we'd been weaving for quite some time, certainly since the time she'd eaten that piece of cake off my fingers during a breakfast we'd consumed in some hotel, in some city I could no longer even remember; or to draw the scenario we were in, painted with increasingly deliberate shades, to its conclusion. I asked myself why I was in that room and not my own, and why that woman, married, with children, gorgeous, had welcomed me into that space and now—I'm guessing—was brushing her teeth, preparing herself for me and for the night ahead. I told myself that it was all happening because she thought of me not as I, in fact, was, but as I'd always wanted to be, and how, to my surprise, in recent years, I was now beginning to really feel. And it occurred to me that if I wanted to hold on to the affection, respect, even the desire Tilde had for me, I'd have to live up to the person who had piqued her sensibility, her intelligence. Tilde came out of the bathroom. She was barefoot, and all she wore was a blue slip. I took her left hand, kissed it devotedly, and passed my tongue across her fragrant palm, which smelled of body cream. I said:

—You're extremely beautiful, and I want you, very much, but I can't go any further. What will happen after tonight? We'll make love, and then? No, I can't cheat on my wife, I love her, I love my kids. I thought I could, but I can't, it's not in me, I'm not made that way.

I said this last bit with the genuine pride of a man in the right. Tilde abruptly withdrew her left hand and slapped me hard in the face with her right. My glasses went flying and landed on the bed. I touched my cheek and felt tears coming to my eyes, and so I escaped her furious gaze with the excuse that I needed to pick up my glasses.

—Good night, I said.

She said quietly:

—Wait, I'm sorry. It was a stupid thing to do, I was wrong, come here.

—No, I said quietly in turn. I'm the one to blame. Let's eat breakfast together, at eight o'clock?

—Yes.

I left and took the stairs down to my room on the third floor. My cheek was burning, but I hadn't lost my footing, I hadn't fallen, if anything, I felt lighter. Everything that seemed solid was made, instead, of an air that sustained my weight, like an airplane in flight, whose route was finally clear. And I was content.

20.

I trace the start of my new life back to that night in Milan, even though, for many years now, I've believed that it's self-deceiving to think of beginnings and endings in terms of ascribed dates. The very next morning, things went remarkably smoothly. Tilde and I had breakfast together, with genuine good cheer, as if the day before, fearing a deadly illness, we'd undergone decisive clinical tests and, now that our bodies had been declared utterly healthy, we were now boldly alive.

On the trip back, we even managed to talk about what had happened between us, and we had a good laugh. At a certain point, however, while she was driving, I turned serious, and traced my finger over the hem of her dress—a boundary that ran quite close to her slender knees—and tried to put words to an impression that I had in mind ever since we'd shut ourselves up in the car. Had we made love, I said, my finger, now, would feel nothing of what that fabric beckons. And she agreed, and we went on to imagine how much our perceptions would have been lost forever if, in the course of that night, we'd gotten to know every square inch of each other, rendering us deaf to each other's details. The list amused us, and there was only one painful moment when Tilde suddenly cried out, just as I was talking about the shape of her small ear, which barely had a lobe and adhered to her nape:

—What idiocy.

—What, no more kidding around?

She shook her head vigorously:

—No, no, keep going. But now I know that the last thing I wanted to do was make love to you.

—Then what did you want?

—I can't explain it without sounding ridiculous.

She uttered that last bit with a twitch of her mouth, all the more surprising if you bear in mind that, up until a few seconds ago, she seemed happy. I wavered, and was about to say, go ahead, be ridiculous, but I decided not to, because I thought of something extremely similar that Teresa had said to me, yelling in the course of one of our fights. We were in the apartment in San Lorenzo. She was trying to tell me something that had to do with her need to be loved, and I'd reduced that need to a sarcastic triviality. She who, even though she went delirious with pleasure every time we made love, said distinctly: hey, excuse me, you really think I'm with you because of that silly little thing you have between your legs, is that what you think? And, in a rage, she started breaking objects, yelling that there was no way to explain herself, not to me who seemed to understand everything, absolutely everything, even the most elusive feelings, even the most ineffable thoughts, but instead I was worse than the dullest of men, I broke the bones and slit the throat of whoever ended up on top of or under me, I was a trap, a trap that was well hidden. She stopped there; her chest heaved audibly. She'd turned blue like wailing children

who can't catch their breath, and I shouted, startled: Teresa,
please, Teresa, what's wrong? And finally her breath returned.

Tilde looked at me for an instant, out of the corner of her
eye. She was waiting for me to say something, but she must
have realized that I'd lost my train of thought, and she murmured, as if speaking to herself: I need to stop for five minutes.
She soon pulled into a service station, vanished to pee, and I
ran to do the same. When we regrouped, she took my hand
with a very focused look on her face, led me over to a patch of
grass close by and said: will you let me sleep for a bit next to
you? She kneeled down, then stretched out on the grass. I
looked around, embarrassed, before lying down beside her;
Tilde, on the other hand, made herself comfortable right away,
resting her head against my shoulder. There was a nice smell of
freshly cut grass battling with the smell of gasoline. I didn't
close my eyes. She slept for almost half an hour close to my
side, resting an arm diagonally across my chest. When she
woke up—abruptly, her eyes disoriented—she said: I feel better now, and we traveled the rest of the way to Rome, all the
way to my building, chatting as usual about this, that, and the
other thing. We said goodbye, vowing to remain friends forever. She only said, jokingly: you can trust me, but as for that
woman in the back of the room, you'd better be careful, take
my advice. Then she called out, as she headed off, to say hello
to Nadia and the children.

I—I must say—couldn't wait to put my arms around my
wife again. I entered the house, on edge, hoping that the desire
I'd had for Tilde hadn't left an evasive look in my eyes, an
unease that Nadia, with the radar of an insecure companion,
might sniff out. But it was nearly midnight, and she was sleeping. She muttered something, still sleeping, without realizing
that I'd come home.

21.

The next day, and then in ways that were increasingly evident in the weeks that followed, I found my wife in good spirits, indeed, affectionate in a way she hadn't been in a long time. At first I worried, afraid that she wanted to have another baby. But it was soon clear to me that she'd put an end to an entire phase of her life, and that she now wanted to stop to enjoy, to the fullest, what she had. In fact, she started describing the university as a remote place filled with seething serpents and scorpions, and talking about the high school as her true place of work. She said this without outward signs of frustration, to the contrary, with each passing day, she grew increasingly adept at managing, without any apparent effort, her teaching alongside her responsibilities to the children. And so, I was forced to realize that the young Nadia was extinct, and that now, in my house and in my bed, there was a stable woman who considered herself an excellent math teacher, a mother who saw after the needs of three children, and a wife who, after a long period of decline, had gone back to looking after herself so as not to look bad next to a husband who'd gained some discreet success.

That about-face reassured me. If Nadia was in a good place, then so were Emma, Sergio, and scrawny little Ernesto. But I, above all, felt great. I could teach, study, talk in public about my book, collaborate with magazines and newspapers, and not fret about creating or exacerbating wounds in the family structure, at the very moment when I was trying to render my public image coherent and possibly invulnerable. Nadia was there, she saw to everything, especially to me, and she was happy to do it.

I didn't ask myself what had so pleasantly altered her, not for lack of interest, but out of caution. Now she kindly kept up with all of my activities as a minor intellectual who, whenever given the chance, had things to say about the importance of the school system, and she relayed to me, frequently with pride, that some colleague of hers, or the friends back in Pratola Peligna, or her parents' friends, had spoken well of one of my books or, who knows, of a recently published article. But I'd noticed that if I overdid it with bragging, even in a joking way, that kindness, and that pride, could reverse course and turn into forced smiles, into a form of withdrawal with the excuse of having something pressing to do. And I even ended up suspecting that certain melancholy spells, certain temporary depressions, might have been an appendix to the moodiness that tales of my success provoked in her. One Saturday morning, I was reading aloud the letter of an academic quite famous at the time, who'd praised a brief piece of mine in the newspaper. Nadia gave half a smile and said:

—He's probably one of Itrò's friends.

—Could be.

—I'm sure he is. Sometimes you forget how much you owe Itrò.

I said, cautiously:

—I'm the one who wrote the article. Not him.

—True, but there are plenty of smart people out there.

—Are you saying that if you read me in a newspaper without Itrò's backing, you wouldn't care about what I said?

—Of course I'd care. But can you say for certain that without Itrò's support, the newspapers would have invited you to write for them?

I admitted that I wasn't certain. But I did that for peace and quiet; I didn't want any friction with her, my days were busy. Our house was becoming a stomping ground: students and teachers would come to visit, even from other cities, and they'd talk to me about their experiences in pedagogy. But people who worked for tiny magazines and publishers would also turn up, people who wanted to have conversations, who wanted to float their ideas, use me for this or that. When it came to female visitors in particular, Nadia turned surly, and afterward she'd say: maybe we really should move, this place is too small, the kids have nowhere to play and I need a space to myself, I don't want to live with all these comings and goings, it's like some seaport. Needless to say, I couldn't turn people away by saying things like: please don't come, my wife starts to sulk, especially if you happen to be chatty young girls or learned female professors speaking with thoughtful cadences. I told her: you're right, as soon as some money comes in, we'll take stock of our finances and move.

Money, to be honest, was coming in, and I was taking serious stock, I often flaunted the figures to show off, eagerly, how our bank account was growing. But that was the very subject that sparked another risky period of high tension. One evening, after dinner, I told her proudly about a bit of money that I'd just received for my books. I said, "I've earned," using the perfect tense, first person singular. She, who had just cleared the table and was now ironing one of my shirts—I was leaving for somewhere the following day, all I did was leave—corrected me without even raising her eyes from the ironing board.

—We've earned. You'd never have written three words without me.

I quickly added:

—Yes, you've been by my side, your presence was crucial.

—Not my presence, what presence are you talking about? I'm talking about my time. The things you write, the places you go off to, your success, your looking so handsome and getting compliments and being celebrated, takes up a boatload of my time.

—Of course, Bertolt Brecht: *On every page a victory. / Who cooked the victory banquet?*

—Cooking's the least of it, a cook's salary would suffice. You owe me a lot more.

I looked at her, perplexed. She was standing in the kitchen, moving the iron back and forth with her eyes lowered. More than anything, she seemed to want to avoid making false folds.

—You're right, I said, cutting it short. I'm sorry. We've earned.

22.

I was beginning to feel more married to Teresa than to Nadia. But maybe that's not the right way of putting it, maybe I should simply specify that my everyday wife kept me less in check than the one overseas, whose eruptions were always a fervid whirlwind of possible salvation and probable ruin. In other words, the new institution that Teresa had jokingly baptized "an ethical marriage" had begun to do its job. Even to the point where she started to write to me without provocation, not to my home address, but to the school. Brief letters at the start, affectionate, one each week, which, to be brutally frank, could have been boiled down to a simple: how's it going? But I read them and reread them, surprised by that about-face, and when I wrote back, I spewed out at least two dense pages, either enthusiastically embracing—or cautiously refuting— whatever it was that she seemed to be saying between the lines.

That epistolary exchange soon became a habit. She narrated, concisely, her news—work-related problems, too little money, boyfriends that lasted a few weeks, the enormous cockroaches in Boston that she found even in her sheets or in the hallway when she went to the bathroom at night—and I, in a more verbose way, told her about me, often asking her advice about some situation or other that was troubling, or about some event that I thought might be an important step for getting ahead.

I don't know if Teresa's epistolary vigilance altered me even more. Certainly, if she herself, in spite of her dreadful personality, ended up sentimentally caving now and then, and admitting—but only burying it within a sentence—that our correspondence was meaningful to her, why shouldn't I at least speculate that, indeed, our matrimonial pact was working out? In those letters, I felt her ever more at my side, even though her tone was quite often incredibly cutting: bravo, who would've guessed that the most egotistical, least sensitive man I know is losing his backbone, is softening?

Obviously, she exaggerated. I had always been a flexible sort of person. But after Milan that flexibility morphed into something more steadily agreeable that—I discovered—yielded excellent results. With my students, for example, I began adopting a pedagogy of fondness that was always increasingly explicit, that is to say, I was considerately dedicating myself to the most fragile, the most rebellious, and to those who seemed less talented. With colleagues, I emphasized politeness and good manners, and I turned much of my attention to those who were, for some reason or other, in the margins. I even began to think that my father-in-law was interesting—the old pedantic principal who always wanted to teach me how to live in the world, even though in reality he'd always lived in the provinces and knew nothing about the world. I myself was surprised that I was starting to think he was interesting, to the point where my mother-in-law once remarked to her daughter: what's happened to your husband, why is he giving in so much to Dad, doesn't it annoy him? But that was the amazing thing: no one annoyed me anymore, annoying people above all. The more time passed, the more I paid attention to all manner of conversation, finding, each time, something to learn, something to suggest.

My sense of bliss also grew—I hazarded to call it that: it was a modest exultance, a discreet joy—with which I faced every public debate. By now I knew that I had a knack with words, but I was no longer anxious about proving it to myself. When others spoke, I refrained from seeming impatient. Instead, I listened, with sincere goodwill, to what everyone had to say, and even on those occasions, I sensed my sympathy for the most aggressive among them, the most hateful, growing inside me. I never missed a beat of what those people said, and they often struck me as people with more substance compared to the pleasant ones. I listened to them with an expression that was, mind you, not one of agreement, not at all, but of understanding, which I expressed with an indistinct sound that's difficult to explain in writing, something that resembled a "u." When all grew silent and it was my turn to speak, I lingered over my notes, I sketched that sonorous scribble one last time in the air, and then I launched into a speech that was critical but always measured, with mild-mannered language that pleased the audience.

One time, I wrote to Teresa to tease her: those couple of hours in the bar in Milan illuminated me; my whole body, finding itself once again next to yours, took stock of our troubled cohabitation, when I tolerated you, each day, a bit less, and my entire being understood—felt—that a loving form of understanding is the only way to cope with unbearable people. Just like that, with a falsely solemn attitude. Naturally, she flew into a rage, showering me with insults, and wrote: think about how unbearable you were, and still are, you imbecile, and how petty and false and cruel, with these little sayings of yours that have always drowned me in a malice that was yours, only yours. She went on to conclude that I should either apologize for what I'd written, or she would withdraw the bridges for good, with all the ensuing consequences.

Reading that reply saddened me. Teresa, in spite of her years and her success, was still the way she was when she was a girl, reactive to everything. In each of my ironic statements, she was convinced that I was set out to harm her, which wasn't at all true, or at least, so I believed, and if I told her, she'd fly into even more of a rage. She was unjustified, and nevertheless, she was convinced of being in the right. I rushed to apologize, I told her that at times I didn't realize what I said. You reproach me—I wrote—and I, look, I amend my ways, I learn. I begged her to keep writing to me, to keep correcting me. If, at times, I'd gotten out of line with her, it was thanks to her, thanks to our correspondence, that in day-to-day life, I no longer did.

23.

That's how it was. At the start, I must admit, I felt I was imitating someone else: a character in a novel or a film whom I no longer remembered; or a real person I'd briefly met when I was young, who had left an impression on me. But at a certain point—and this was a new thing in my life—I ended up telling myself: no, at last, now that I'm nearly forty years old, this sensitivity and this intelligence belong to me.

Something specific happened one night, in the same neighborhood on the outskirts where my school was located, in a bleak little auditorium. It was a defining episode. The usual debate was in store, but when I got there, I sensed that things were going to get complicated: the person who had invited me had greeted me with hostility, but above all, beside me at the table, I saw the same individual who, a long time ago, had panned my first book in a handful of sentences, and immediately afterward, had gotten up and left.

Recognizing him made me very uncomfortable. It was he who presented me to the audience: mothers of families with restless children, retired people, some students, and a few of my colleagues from school. According to the general rules of conduct, he should have just said a few words, but instead he spoke for much longer than expected, behaving as if he were the real protagonist of the evening. And above all, instead of singing my praises, which was what typically happened on such occasions, he analyzed my books, punctiliously, along with a few recent articles, speaking of what they lacked. It's a matter, in the end, of meaningless commonplaces, he finally said, with all the sarcasm he could muster.

He had a conspicuous number of supporters in the room, and once or twice a little laughter or a giggle rose up, a clapping of hands. I stared at the fabric that covered the table, without missing a word he said. The material was an irritating lilac shade that, under a few old neon lights, now turned to the shade of blood, now to a purple, like an elongated bruise. Once or twice, I felt dizzy and feared I would fall off the chair, but I continued to listen, attentively, without any outward show of discomfort.

It really was a critical moment. I had to hold the impact of the insults in check, and the anger, and the desire to react in a violent way. That large man, of indefinable age, with a fat neck, the long thin gap between his meager lips, was spitting venom with evident satisfaction. He was so overwhelmed by malevolence that even his sweat seemed poisonous to me, and the smell he emanated. Nevertheless, I realized that the thing to do was give him time: the more he talked, the more I inoculated myself; the more the lava that ran through my chest cooled, the more I perceived the basis of his suffering. He taught law; his name was Franco. Someone at the start of the evening had called him Franchino. He had a black spot on the nail of his right thumb, as if it had gotten jammed in a door. He directed the greater part of his speech not toward the audience but to me, as if what he really cared about was making sure that I understood how hostile he was. Which was maybe why I was so struck by the paleness of his face, compared to the red in his eyes, and not the details of what he was saying. Moreover, here, now, the quality of his critique didn't matter. He kept insisting, using increasingly aggressive methods, on one thing in the end: if the State paid teachers shit, teachers had to repay with shitty performances. The rest flowed from that proposition. Above all, he deduced that whoever preached the need for a job well done—me, for instance—was a servant. A servant, he said, fixing me with his red eyes, the servant of principals, superintendents, ministers. A servant of the mechanism that exploits to the gills any kind of work, paying next to nothing. After that he said nothing else, and he received a huge round of applause, and to everyone's surprise, my own above all, I, too, applauded him, firmly, and was the last to stop. The man looked at me, confused. He dried his shiny mouth with the back of his hand, gave a perfidious smile, looked at the wristwatch he'd placed on the table half an hour before and said, though without apologizing: I've over-spoken.

Thank goodness he over-spoke, I thought with genuine relief. Thank goodness, because if he'd only spoken for five minutes we'd have come to blows. Instead, in the course of that long half-hour, I had been able to discern his unhappiness. It was an unhappiness I knew, that of an individual—a spasm of living matter in the form of a human organism—in front of a device that was poorly projected, poorly executed, poorly reformed—the lecture hall, the school, the teaching—which, in the beginning, appears correctable, only a small defect, but then expands to the whole scholastic institution, the family, the organization of collective life in all its incredibly precarious forms. That unhappiness touched me, and I was almost afraid of getting emotional when, after the audience's applause for Franchino, I began to talk, to declare that I agreed with him, that I also agreed with the fierce criticism he had dealt me, and to tell everyone, in my own words, of the desperation I had just perceived. Terrible, I said, condensing aloud pages from both my books, and disheartening, to be responsible for budding lives, and feel that one expects everything of you without you getting anything in return, and to know every day that you're increasingly unheard. You write about the people you owe your discomfort to, and no one reads you, you denounce the conditions you work in and no one notices, you scream and no one hears, everything remains as it is, unresolved, in your lecture hall and in the world, so that exhaustion sets in and you say who gives a fuck, bring on the catastrophe, let everything go to hell, when we hit bottom we'll feel the impact, and then the sparks will finally fly, iron to iron, and everything will go up in flames, and then we'll rebuild the right way. But meanwhile, as we wait for that to happen, life goes by, and goes by ever more debased, ours and those of the children who parade past us year after year, and we never really hit bottom, debasement yes, old age yes, death yes, but never the bottom, no, it can always get worse. Therefore, I concluded, I'll tell you how I see it. I don't want to feel like I have to declare that the best would still be the best even if I weren't their teacher, and the worst are still the worst even though I'm their teacher. Shitty pay or not, forthcoming apocalypse or not, I want to say, here, quietly, that I feel less sad—yes, less sad—if I work like a slave because the ones who would do well anyway do better thanks to my work, and because those who would, in any case, do poorly learn to do better thanks to me. I don't mean to reduce myself along with my students to a ground zero of teaching. Human beings reduced to argh, ugh, and ooh ooh ooh are never promising. Therefore, dear colleague, let's try to keep our unhappiness at bay, and let's react, not with the roar of gorillas that incites revolts or, if you like, revolutions, etcetera, etcetera. I went on like this, clear and concise, not for more than fifteen minutes, often touching the arm of that teacher of law who detested me, Franchino, even taking his hand at one point, the one that had the painfully marked thumb. I felt as if he were someone I'd sat next to in class since first grade, constrained since then in a classroom, as if in a jail cell, victims of the exact same reclusion. They were fifteen truly amazing minutes, for how I felt close to the truth of things, for the way my heart was beating. When I stopped talking, it was the mothers and the students who seemed to agree most of all.

Franchino, in contrast, got up suddenly. He headed for one side of the room, he seemed irritated even by the throng of his supporters. I hoped, to myself, that I hadn't hurt him on any level, and rather, when the chatter with mothers and fathers and grandparents had ended, and workers who worried about the future of their children and grandchildren, I sidled up on purpose, politely nodding goodbye. This, I realized, must have seemed beyond the pale to him. Me? Say goodbye? To him? He looked over at me, amazed, with a kind of shudder caught between hostile gloom and the anxious desire to say something to me right away—anything—provided that the hour we'd spent in front the audience, side by side, would not vanish without an extra something, however vague, even half a misplaced sentence.

—You're heading out?

—Yes, it's late.

—Wait a minute.

—Okay.

He gathered his overcoat and followed me into the street, up to my car. He said quietly:

—You were upset.

—About what?

—I took it too far, and I don't even know why. I feel this resentment inside, for god knows how long, but believe me, it's not like me, at least it's not how I'd like to be, and tonight, while you were talking, the whole time I asked myself: what drove me to say what I said, to use the words I did, where did that come from? I'm sorry.

—You don't need to apologize. You said things that made me think.

I spoke to him without rhetorical flourishes, or at least that's how it felt to me in that moment, and I felt better. Even his remorse, the confused repentance, felt like my own, and I was pleased by it. I shook Franchino's hand, I gave him my phone number. I urged him: get in touch, let's get together, let's find time to keep talking.

In brief, I emerged from that evening not only satisfied with myself, which was by now what usually happened, but with a sense of stability. I'd always been afraid that my attachment to every word—nothing off-base, no divergence—was, as Teresa always reminded me, a fragile thing. After that experience, on the other hand, it seemed really quite unlikely that I would ever revert to being as I once was: disorganized, off the mark, off-balance, indecent, a cheater if need be. Rather, I thought that the combined threat and salvation, constituted by Teresa, was only an imaginative way for us to stay in touch, but one that, in fact, had no influence on our natures, almost surely not on mine. That is, I went on to tell myself—an entirely new fact—maybe, for reasons that annoyed me to think about, I'd misrepresented myself from the beginning, and had always, potentially, been devoted to good, maybe I'd simply undergone a distortion in the early part of my life, which can happen to anyone, to men both great and minor, nothing serious, we all ended up getting back on track. And so, I told myself—and meanwhile, also wrote about it to Teresa, as if she really were a beloved wife to whom one confides every thought and feeling—from now on, my goal isn't purely and simply to hew to the right path and not slip off it, that's no longer enough; now I want to be, always, the way I was in that auditorium on the outskirts: a perfect I, so perfectly joined that it would dovetail with me completely.

24.

I tried to live up to that end. Nadia, meanwhile—set to work on our moving to a new place, in cahoots with Tilde and Itrò, and egged on largely by the wife of the latter, Ida: a pianist of discreet technical skill but very frequent professional engagements, painfully thin, and always dressed in black, as if she were already a widow. My wife had, for once and for all, become another person: from bearing three children, she had emerged, timidly at first, but then with growing determination, as a woman charged with energy, extremely cordial with my friends and acquaintances, and ready to display her practical side. Thanks to her, we left the apartment way out on Via Nomentana and rented another on the banks of the Tiber, in Flaminio, not too far from the luxurious dwelling of Mr. and Mrs. Itrò. After the initial difficulties, things got better, and even Emma, Sergio, and Ernesto, for whom the move had been hard, were convinced that our situation had improved. Now we lived in a place full of light. The two boys shared a nice big room, and Emma had a small one to herself. Nadia chose a room that overlooked the Tiber as her studio; I carved out some space on a meager enclosed veranda that looked out on a terrace, and beyond its railing, I could gaze out at antennas, terra-cotta roof tiles, and chimneys, or alternatively, my eyes would drop down into the deep, dark well of a little cloister.

For a while, we kept teaching at our school on the outskirts, but then that became onerous. Now we had to wake up at five-thirty, and even that wasn't early enough, given the complicated needs of the family. But Itrò took this to heart, and soon found a way to transfer me to a prestigious high school in the center, and my wife to a technical school right by our apartment. And so it happened that, not without some melancholy, I left behind the school where I'd been teaching since I was twenty-five years old, where I'd met sixteen-year-old Teresa, where I'd been her teacher for three years, and where I'd met Nadia, back when she still dreamed of teaching at a university.

At the new school, I was welcomed with politeness, then with hostility, and in the end, quite soon, amiably. Naturally, with a few teachers and small groups of students, the enmity persisted, or rather, it tended to flare up when I published some article ranting at those who, either in a programmed way or for personal insufficiency, on all levels of the hierarchy, did a sloppy job of working or studying. But soon something happened, one of the many events that, back then, surprised me more than anyone. Franchino, about whom I'd by then forgotten, gave me a call. We got together, we had a beer, we talked a long while, and after that, he stopped by to see me every other week. We got to know each other quite well; he even showed up a few times at the school. And it was at the school that I discovered how famous he was, and incredibly revered for his commitment to union politics, above all by those who, as soon as I gave them cause, would criticize me harshly. These people couldn't believe that Franchino deigned to chat with me in the atrium. Someone came forward, making respectful overtures, and began to listen in, and then another, later, asked me, disoriented: you know him? You're friends? And there was confusion for a while. Who was I? A reactionary, a fellow traveler, or a real comrade? A few rushed to lift me out of my pigeonhole into their political and cultural one, others would grant me this upgrade only when Franchino, with just a few generous words, gave heft to what I wrote, and to me, in public. And so, after not too long, I felt completely at ease at the new school and, I must say, also getting along swimmingly with my former detractor.

I told Teresa, in the letters we continued to write each other, lots about Franchino. She replied by reminding me of how my great friendships in the past had all met with a terrible end. I had told her myself how quickly they'd developed, and how, just as quickly, they'd fizzled out. As a matter of fact, a few times, she'd been witness both to the first phase as well as the second. And she was right, that bond between me and Franchino was nothing new. I'd always aroused, in both sexes, a need for an indissoluble bond. Ever since I was a boy, I'd been considered indispensable; playmates and friends would want me all to themselves, they'd hound me. But then what would happen? It was as if everyone, each in a different way, got scared of how strong our bond was, and out of the blue, from being all too present, they turned into shades in my memory. Girls would turn this into a tragedy, so that most of my love affairs had ended in extremely painful separations. The males, on the other hand, tended to say abruptly, with no clear motive: it's best we stop seeing each other.

This tendency had wounded me, and I'd always been wary of it. I felt like a book that people raved about at the start, but then, little by little, started to satisfy less, or even went downhill. My mother—my own mother, no less—hadn't she behaved this same way? I'd been her favorite, but in a family where love wasn't enough to erase the suffering. My father believed she was unfaithful—he'd had that fixation—and constantly yelled at her; she would reply, yelling back in turn: it's not true, you're crazy, you see things that don't exist. I was so distressed by the affliction of both of them that I set about, early on, to distance them, to make them fade, to erase my love for them and, without realizing it, for anyone. My thoughts, I recall, even at the age of eight or nine, were cold-blooded. If she's a whore, I said to myself, he shouldn't just yell at her, he should kill her. And if she's not, he needs to stop tormenting her, or I'll grab the bread knife and kill him in his sleep. I saw the blood now of one, now the other, but without emotions, from afar. Once, in the kitchen, in our wretched kitchen in Naples, in the forties or start of the fifties, in the previous century, my mother had read something in my eyes, or maybe in the way my lips were twisted, and she told me I frightened her. I was frightening? Me? They were the ones who frightened me. How I'd suffered for what she'd said, but I'd squelched that suffering in my heart, to the point of suffocating it. Sometimes I'd circle around my mother to see if she'd caress me, but I don't recall that she ever did.

But by the 1980's, no one wanted to retreat from me. My three children were always by my side, people started to read what I'd written and what I was writing, Itrò was deeply fond of me, Tilde cared for me deeply, my new home welcomed the young and the old, men and women, all of them admired me, and for each, it was a struggle to bid me farewell. And then Franchino—he who, in the past had actually hated me—held on to me tight. When he'd come over, he made a habit of leaving at least an hour after the other guests. Once he asked me, on the q.t.:

—What about women? Do you know how many I'd have, if I were you?

—I don't have any lovers.

—Never?

—Never.

—Not even one of these respectable ladies or young girls always buzzing around you?

—No one. I'm faithful to my wife.

He gave me a long, questioning look, unsure of whether or not to ask his next question.

—And your wife? he finally asked.

—What about my wife?

—Is your wife faithful to you?

25.

I didn't like the question. Nadia did all she could to fit into the increasingly complex scenario around me, and I appreciated this, but there was an excess of solicitousness in her that disturbed me. I mean, it mattered so much to her to highlight how well our lives had gone that at times I thought: she's lying to herself; she doesn't think things are going well at all. One day she was happy about my ongoing success, the following day she thought that the possibility of my collaborating with, say, an important newspaper would constitute a problem for our family, one that she was aware of but that I, obtusely, was not. So I stuck to evading both her cheerfulness and her bad moods, until it suddenly became clear that she really would appreciate the entirety of my very fortunate ascent, but only on the condition that I remained, paradoxically, the middling teacher she had fallen in love with.

To put it more clearly, my wife was worried about the person I was becoming. Her old alarm bells, triggered by new developments that would now and then blindside me, were now keener. She regarded my success as a threat to our marriage, a threat to the children, and above all, an insult to her: I, who had never been ambitious, who had been rewarded by destiny, and she, who'd had many ambitions, and had been left behind without being able to show me that she was a bright star in her field. Well then, what to say? It was as if Nadia didn't feel that any decorations had been pinned on her chest, and therefore, in order to prevent our relationship from going off-balance and down the drain, wanted to pull mine off me. At times, it seemed as if she monitored me only to gather proof that my advantages were unmerited. If she didn't do her work as well as I did, if she wasn't able to appear in public as winningly as I did, if even Emma, Sergio, and Ernesto adored me more than they adored her, it was the halo I insisted on wearing on my head that was to blame. I sensed her aggression, her tenderness, her coldness, her overbearingness, and I suffered for the way her instability made her suffer. But I literally had so much to do that I never found the time to minimize her suffering.

But ignoring matters never works out well. At a certain point, I had to take stock of a few unusual behaviors on her part. Due to a long-standing habit, I would talk to her at length about people I admired, and she, for the most part, paid me scant attention. But from a certain point onward, on the contrary, anyone who admired me, and whom I admired back, became someone worthy of her total attention. The person who formed part of this canon aroused her curiosity, and she would dress up for him, she'd launch into long, animated conversations, and she'd laugh a lot, she'd listen to him, looking devoutly into his eyes. There was no need for anyone new to turn up, to dazzle her with his charms. It even happened with Itrò. And Itrò went crazy, he couldn't believe that after years of knowing us, all of a sudden, this gorgeous, intelligent woman was paying him so much attention, and that she wanted to go on walks with him—a skinny balding guy, a bit bumbling—that she wanted to go to the movies, to the theatre, to a concert. Before this sudden rise in familiarity between the two of them, Mrs. Itrò, dressed in black, became darker still, proceeding to make stinging remarks and then waiting it out, hoping that I would pry her husband's skinny thigh away from my wife's soft and silky one.

But I didn't lift a finger. What do you want to do—Teresa wrote, making fun of me—confront the petty pedagogue, slap him, challenge him to a duel, wait for him in a dark corner so you can slit his throat? Think about it. Is Itrò putting the moves on your wife, groping her against her will? No. It's the other way around. And even if he does, while you're reading this letter, do you really want to get into it with him? He'd be guilty of the same thing you've committed a hundred times, with women who were married or otherwise taken, even when we were together, and you were supposed to be faithful to me.

So shut up and relax. And wake up to the situation: your wife, with all likelihood, is ready to get into bed with anyone who thinks highly of you, in order to prove that they think even more highly of her, while your admirers are ready to go to bed with her in order to feel less humiliated by the greatness they unreasonably attribute to you.

As usual, she was ironic, often sarcastic; Teresa was always ribbing. But in that moment, I took her words seriously, and I believed she was right. Nadia grew intimate not with whomever came along, but with people I frequented and openly esteemed, people, mind you, who were physically unattractive: scholars worn down by study, teachers tuckered out by their robust didactic endeavors. Look at what's gone and happened to you, my former student wrote me, sarcastically: you, a man who's over six feet tall, with your thick golden hair, the forest of your sex, also golden, with sky-blue eyes and long, mysteriously dark lashes, you are now so very loved and desired that, to seek your attention, to have you, the insignificant people allow themselves to be penetrated, and penetrates you by means of another person.

But the thesis didn't hold up, it was Teresa herself who struck it down. She changed her tone, in fact, she wrote: enough with these secondhand psychological truisms; as usual, the real problem is you. And then she went on: you always said you weren't jealous, but you're lying, you lie without shame, you want the right to cheat all to yourself, and if someone cheats on you, then watch out, even the mere thought drives you insane. Do you think I've forgotten how you once tormented me? So she began to defend my wife: Nadia just wants to be welcoming and kind, but you're sick in the head and see things that don't exist; you'd better behave.

In certain letters, she really did want to help me face the situation with poise, but in others she got angry, she threatened me, and her sentences, sent from across the ocean, tormented

me like the voice of a cruel ghost. It was in the course of that
confused seesaw that my childhood returned, and adolescence, the worst moments of my past, and that barely concealed aversion toward myself resurfaced. I'll do what I need
to do, I now began to think, I'll find a lover, I'll respond to
betrayal with betrayal. But I quickly felt depressed, I chased
that idea away, and I urged myself: let's get down to brass
tacks, what does an eye for an eye change, the problem is
whether Nadia really is betraying me or not. And so, before my
eyes that worked like magnifying glasses, there came to pass a
series of friendly signs, affectionate words, excessive attentive-
ness, a desire that cloaked itself behind cordially cheerful
tones. And still, zero glaring proof of adultery. Once, when I
was out of my mind, I wrote to Teresa: if I find out that Nadia
is cheating on me, followed by three dots. I received a long,
gloating letter in which she said, in just a few words: say what
you mean, what does that ellipsis signify, do you mean that if
she cheats on you, you'll kill her? Yes, maybe, I wrote back
almost on the heels of her letter. When I was a boy, that's what
I'd wordlessly suggested to my father, so why shouldn't I suggest the same thing to myself, now that I was an adult? And
Teresa, after a long pause, wrote back, this time without a playful tone, without sarcasm, without invective, but serious: don't
you even dare think of it, otherwise, you know what will happen to you.

Yes, that I knew. I trained myself to contemplate Nadia's
frenzy and suffocate my guesswork in the dark. But meanwhile, I feared that, by means of repressing myself, the impas-
siveness of my late childhood would return, when my mother
would flee from the house yelling that she wanted to throw
herself out the window, and my father would run after her,
showering her with insults, and I would cut out paper figures,
without getting distracted for even a second, methodically
drawing eyes, mouths, checkered shirts, pants, boots, and belts

with cowboy guns, as if nothing were going on around me. No, regressing scared me, I wanted to find a new state of equilibrium, I wanted to think carefully. I had taken it upon myself to be a reliable husband, and Nadia was perhaps turning into an unreliable wife. But could I really pit my faithfulness, with good reason, against the possibility of my wife's infidelity? No. My fidelity didn't depend on my love for her but—I admitted this to myself—was the result of another, more robust fidelity, the one to Teresa. In fact, the more time passed, the more I seemed to have a deep bond with that woman who lived far away, one I hadn't even seen for years. By now, as a joke to myself, I'd call her my phantom consort. And what was Nadia? A lady who regretted what I'd been and, in order to not be crushed by my real weight, gave weight to others. Teresa, on the other hand, didn't abandon me even for a minute. Even if she lived and worked with a series of her own successes on various continents, she never got distracted, she always kept me with the bit in my mouth, brushing my coat, grooming me, giving me sugar cubes, lathering me up, and by doing so, she was aiming to make me the perfect man she'd wanted long before, a man I wasn't.

The truth was, I was Nadia's husband, and that fact made me sometimes feel ridiculous, like any husband, and also provoked a pain so severe that I always felt increasingly at risk, as if I were a worm-ridden artifact. Some of our conversations upset me. I wanted to slam doors, shatter things. Instead, I ended up only running myself down.

—Where were you?

—At the bookstore.

—The one in the neighborhood?

—In Trastevere.

—Four hours in a bookstore dressed like a showgirl?

—It was for the book talk of one of Stefano's friends.

Stefano was, of course, Itrò, whom we all referred to at

home by his last name, even the children: only Nadia, recently, had started to call him by name, with a sort of languid satisfaction.

—Why didn't you tell me about it?

—I thought you knew.

—I didn't. But if you'd told me, we could have gone together.

—Maybe Stefano only wanted to invite me.

—Or maybe you wanted to go alone.

—And what if I did? Could you, for once, give me a little space, please?

—I give you far too much.

—You? You occupy every single slot and I can't have my own life.

—What does your own life mean? A life without me?

—So now you're jealous?

—Of Itrò? Let's not kid ourselves, Itrò is a father to me.

—You've always hated your father.

—What are you talking about? What do you know about when I was a kid, a teenager? Look, just forget about it, ok? How was the book talk?

—The writer was as bland as a piece of steamed fish, but Stefano was magnificent.

—Obviously.

—Yes.

At a certain point, so as not to break down, I thought I needed to do something. So I stopped, for starters, praising anyone too generously in my wife's presence. By now I was too beyond reproach, in all of my guises, to place anxiety on myself, and onto my own thoughts, and so, now and then, I let myself indulge in harsh judgments, and malicious gossip, even with regards to Itrò, of whom, all told, I was fond. At the same time, I learned to cloud my vision. In general I saw far off, I was always rummaging inside myself, or behind the faces of others. Instead I forced myself to be a little blind, so that I would feel better myself, and to let other people, to let Nadia, feel better. But what to say, I'm a lucky man. Certain cutting comments, tempered by a good-natured absentminded pretending all was fine, generated even more affection around me, even more respect. In that phase, Franchino, above all, glommed on like never before. And Nadia immediately glommed onto him. It was in her presence one afternoon that Franchino proposed that I join a small, aggressive leftist party, of which he was a prominent member. The idea—he explained to me—was to run as a team in the upcoming elections.

—What a couple! Nadia exclaimed.

Two of the buttons on her shirt were undone. I looked at her, frowning. She pretended not to feel my reproachful eyes on the skin of her breasts.

26.

The pain, in that phase, wore me down. I was afraid of breaking apart into a million tiny repugnant pieces. And yet things just kept getting better. At school; on the publishing front; at the talks I gave which were always crowded, always lively; even the complicated political process that would bring me into Parliament—this was what Franchino hoped for, and perhaps what I also hoped for when I wowed people in the course of a televised debate. But there was little to be done, discontent always lurked in a corner, ready to regain ground. What was true—in my thoughts and in my hands, in my fingers, in my legs that were crossed, as I wrote the umpteenth piece on the fate of the school system, on the devastating effects of inequality, on love as the most effective form of pedagogy? True in the sense that I absolutely believed it, not like someone who reads a novel or watches a film, utterly engaged, and yet aware that it's all made up.

One morning, when I had a slight fever, I didn't go to school. I felt listless. I looked at the terrace on the other side of the glass of my tiny veranda, at the roofs, pigeons, crows, gulls, and sky. It was cloudy, and I searched for a thought that would shore me up. What came to mind was: until now things have gone well, but it's above all with my children that I've proven myself. But this thought didn't lift my spirits. How had I proven myself to Emma, Sergio, Ernesto? Had I convinced them of a truth, or a lie? Was I congratulating myself because I had fully revealed myself to them, or because I'd hidden myself just as fully?

I hoped I had nothing more to hide. I was most assuredly a good man, even though, with Teresa, I always had to stay on my toes, there was always the danger that she'd step in and demolish everything—the same thing that happens to those chalk drawings on the sidewalk when it rains and pedestrians mix up all the colors with their shoes, folding in water and filth. A while back, she'd attacked me because I'd recklessly confessed my repulsion toward Franchino and Nadia to her. I'd replied by explaining my reasons, but then I'd grown exasperated and written: you can't fault me for my fantasies as well, sometimes you make me so incredibly angry that I no longer want to slit my wife's throat, but get on a plane and come to slit yours. For weeks, no comment. No big deal, Teresa never wrote much, she often disappeared. At last a letter arrived, and a terrible fight exploded, that had seemingly nothing to do with my gory outburst, but with a trifling matter. She'd told me, some time before, that she'd be touring Europe to attend a series of conferences, and I'd replied: tell me where you'll be and I'll join you. That was what had caused her to kick back: what did I mean by that, join her why, with what right, who was I to her, and she to me, you have your life and I have mine, what do you want, how dare you threaten me, not only is there no love between you and me, but no hate. Between you and me there's nothing at all. She never wrote to me again.

I missed her now. I missed her especially on dull days, like that morning when I was feverish and my thoughts were muddled. I'd recently quit smoking, I no longer drank coffee, I'd even stopped drinking the usual glass of wine with dinner. These small deprivations had become a way, recently, to keep myself in check, especially when, all of a sudden, I would think about my story—and not so much about what had happened to me, about all that I'd satisfyingly accomplished, but about my very awareness of being alive. About I, if you can say that: this personal pronoun that had slipped into the cogs of the universe like an iron bolt—and I asked myself what was the point of my governing life, teaching it good manners, educating it. What earthly gain or heavenly reward was worth refining it with such struggle? I started to get sleepy. I looked at my watch, it was eleven thirty-five, Nadia and the children were in their respective classrooms. An autumn wind was blowing, and I went out onto the terrace even though I felt cold. I glanced up at the sky, full of white clouds and peaceful wisps, then I looked down, leaning over. Who knew where Teresa was, in which of the world's cities. Up until that moment, yes, I was a lucky man, and a good part of my fortune had come from her, even if she frightened me more and more. I thought: what if she burst in now and gave me a shove?

THE SECOND STORY

1.

I'm a problem. I'm one by character, by dint of the upbringing I had, and by vocation. The combination of these three things, over the years, sent two husbands running, procured the tepid love and ever-raging hatred of my four daughters—I only had girls—and turned me into the bane of all the newsrooms I've ever worked for and the delight of readers who love frontline journalists. I realized I'd be a complication again when someone dear to me, whose name and public charge I'll say nothing about, told me that a national day dedicated to schools of all stripes and categories had been added to the calendar, and that a commission created for this purpose, by the office of the president of Italy, was drafting a list of professors, and singling out three who would be awarded prizes on the occasion.

I must admit that, had it been merely a propaganda maneuver by our government, I'd have never paid attention to this bit of news. But first of all, the president was involved, a man I admire, who embodies one of the rare types of masculine old age that warms my heart. And then, I immediately felt proud of being the daughter of not one but two teachers who, in addition to me and my brothers, admirably raised an impressive number of boys and girls destined, without their guidance, to become deadbeats, through the ranks. So I said to my friend:

—Did they already make the list?

—I don't know.

—Can you find out?

—It won't be easy.

—Please do me this for me.

—I'll try.

—If the list is ready, I want it.

He found out, and handed me a list a few hours later, with twenty-eight names on it. I skimmed it with curiosity, perhaps even with some apprehension, and I discovered that just about everyone was on it: mothers of politicians and famous actors, fathers of directors and writers, aunts of well-known cooks on television. Just not my parents. That was when the rabble-rouser in me got in gear, and I barraged my informant with a whirl of quarrelsome demands. He was a bit ticked off, and when we said goodbye he said to me once again: I've always been on your side, Emma, but you can't go nuts over every last thing. And anyway, if you need to get someone into trouble, leave me out of it.

The way he talked to me made me even angrier. List in hand, I verified that indeed, with the exception of a few people I knew well and who had done truly noteworthy things for the school system, the sole merit of each of the others was having given birth to, or in some cases being related to, the conceited charlatans and minor divas of the moment. So I picked up the phone and called the secretary to the president. Luisa, the person I usually dealt with, wasn't in, and someone I'd never head of answered. I said: I have your list of pseudo-instructors in hand, and it's shameful, Pietro Vella isn't on it. The little parrot I was talking to asked: who's Pietro Vella? I asked to speak right away to the president. The person replied: the president has no time to waste. The president, I then said, isn't an imbecile like you. He knows who I am, so he'll be glad to talk to me. In any case, either put me on the phone with him now, or your list, is going to run in the newspapers tomorrow. Then, instead of waiting for an answer, I ended the conversation. I know how to deal with people like that.

Two minutes later, Luisa called, and apologized, and asked

politely, Emma, would you like to tell me what's going on? I explained that I couldn't care less about the list of twenty-eight, that they could choose whomever they wanted, but that I thought it entirely legitimate that, among the three teachers who had added luster to Italian education, there should be perhaps not both my parents, but at least my father who now, sure, was eighty years old, and retired for more than fifteen, but had been an extremely distinguished teacher, greatly admired, and had written two incredibly important books about the school system.

—What's your father's name?

—Luisa, don't be sly, his name is Vella, like mine.

—First name.

—Pietro. And don't tell me you don't know who he is. You're sixty years old, you should remember.

—Sure, I remember, but time passes, things change, and if someone today says Vella, I think of Emma, not Pietro. Refresh my memory. He's written books?

—Two, widely read.

—I'll jot down his name and see if they'll put him on the list for you.

—So the list of twenty-eight will then become twenty-nine?

—Yes.

—Luisa, my father deserves to be one of the three that receive the prize.

—For that there's a selection process, and the president himself has dictated the criteria.

—Let's hear the criteria.

She listed them for me, and they were, objectively, rigorous. Among other things—she explained to me at the end, probably citing from some document—the presence of a student of unimpeachable prestige at the ceremony would be a deciding factor: this person would have to speak, praising the person who educated and trained him or her.

For a few seconds I remained silent. Then I said:

—Have you ever heard of Teresa Quadraro?

—The scientist?

—Brava, she's someone you know. Put my father on the list. He was her teacher.

2.

Luisa has always dealt with people who are more powerful and overbearing than I am, so she didn't let this intimidate her. Whereas I myself, to be truthful, was soon ashamed of having giving her some attitude. What motivated me was, clearly, a private interest, not unlike that of the children and grandchildren who had forced the names of their parents and grandparents onto that list. So the phone call ended with reciprocal declarations of respect: I apologized for being impetuous, but meanwhile hoped for a serious enforcement of the selection criteria, and she asked for some bullet points on my father, and promised to champion him to the selection committee.

I stared for a while at the computer screen. I was in a bad mood. As usual, I'd reacted heedlessly. I shouldn't have exposed myself, I should have found someone who would have been able to propose my father's candidacy after outlining, authoritatively, his merits. Instead, I'd hopped onto the phone without thinking, and now I was forced to assume that Luisa was already talking about me in the way I hate most: as usual, Vella flipped out, I don't know who she thinks she is, she likes to point her finger at everyone and talk them down, and instead she pulls strings and begs for favors like anyone else.

I pulled strings? I asked for favors? All I needed now was for my father to get word that I was pulling strings and begging for favors so that he would receive a stupid prize, and this would have made him suffer greatly. But now what should I do? Say nothing, let it go, avoid going to bat so that his merits would be recognized? No, I should, I told myself. This, too, would cause him pain. He'd always fought so that merits would never be overlooked, especially those infinitesimal ones that were, nevertheless, the fruit of incredible labors. So why shouldn't I insist that now, in his old age, his merits, too, should be recognized, merits that were immense and indisputable?

I wouldn't have to invent anything, indeed, I wouldn't have to blow anything out of proportion at all. My father really had been an excellent teacher, I was wrong to feel embarrassed, it was right to plead his case. Teresa Quadraro, sure, she had the vibe of a famous scientist, and she'd be unassailable proof of the excellent work he'd done. But what to say about all the other students, the ones who would come to the house—as if it were a pilgrimage—even after they graduated, for years, for decades? I remembered so many, I'd seen them ever since I was a little girl, when I was a teenager, up until I'd moved out of the house. Their gratitude had left a mark on me. I hated my teachers—incompetent slackers with extreme swings of temper—and after I graduated from highschool, I was careful not to pay tribute to them not even once, not even for a second. So just imagine the effect, in those days, of that extended gratitude, that untarnished devotion. Recently, it so happened that I'd gone to pay my parents a visit just when one of his former students, one I'd seen when I was a girl, a handsome dark-haired boy who was now graying and nearing sixty, had stopped by to say hello and have a chat with his old teacher. I had a peek; he was hanging on my father's words as if he were still a schoolboy. Well, summoning up that image now, while I was in front of the computer, was crucial. My mood didn't lift, it was still dark and stormy, but my opinion shifted. I'd been right in making Luisa realize, with the necessary aggression, that the question of that prize meant a lot to me. Rather, maybe

I should have also told her that I, myself, wanted to meet with the president. Seriously, as soon as possible. Not that I know him well, I've only interviewed him a few times: years ago, once regarding a political situation, and the other time about grief. And it was on that second occasion that we got to know each other. Luisa was there, she was the one who'd arranged for me to receive a thank you card for my fine work when the interview came out. Which is why I think that if I made her say: Emma Vella would like to talk to you, he'd find the time, and say, all right. Rather, deep down I anticipated another nice thing. The president and my father are the same age, they have the same heft to them, the name Pietro Vella should be one he knows. So it would be easy for me to explain that my request wasn't the gushing gesture of a daughter, but an objectively worthy one. My father, Mr. President, was a teacher for over forty years. My father, Mr. President, was a contributor prized by important newspapers. My father, Mr. President, was an exceptional student. My father, Mr. President, was a passionate politician. My father, Mr. President, really was called upon, more than once, to weigh in on various attempts to reform the school system, and I could name several dull, gray, extremely damaging public education ministers who have sought him out.

I stopped there. My father was: this reiterated perfect tense brought tears to my eyes. I'd never had to use it so pointedly. Usually, when I think of him, it's in an ongoing present. That's how it is even if I remember something from decades ago, when he was always leaving for somewhere—he was often leaving—or came back tired and nevertheless always found time for me, and for my brothers. His carriage as a young man, very tall, brightened by a light that shone from him as if hidden in his blond hair and in his eyes, even from his fingernails, never faded from my eyes, it's still part of *right now*, and right now I suffer from solitude and fragility the way I did when he would go away, and right now I feel happy and invulnerable the way

I did when he would come back. But the indisputable fact is that my father's entire life is now in the past tense; he behaved such that the prestige he acquired didn't last, didn't accompany him into his old age. And so I realized that if, standing before the president, I only listed all that he had done, he wouldn't have understood a thing about his life. I'd have to also list, immediately afterward, seated before him in a light blue and gold armchair, all that my father had refused to do. The president, in fact, would surely have asked me, even if intimated by a glance: why did this this incredibly talented man stop? He would ask this because he, the president, has never stopped, the poof being that he's the president today, and my father isn't. He's at home, being not much of anyone. At that point I would have struggled to explain that it's a question of morality. My father was the most politely willing and able man on earth. Teaching? He taught. Writing books? He wrote them. Writing for the papers? He wrote for them. Politics and the skills to get elected? He turned political and had the skills to get elected. Consulting for the most enlightened of ministers, or almost the most? He consulted for them. He always threw himself into each of these activities with a kind heart and keen intelligence, a formula he greatly loved, and passed on to me. I, too, use it for the rare people who deserve it. But he also retreated with the same politeness, at the first blemish, at the first sign of swindling, at the first request for servile yielding. And he did this without arrogance, rather, by showing great understanding for the suffering of all those who agreed to sully themselves with the world, or at least dirtied themselves as much as they needed to, slaving away without nothing but vulgar pleasures in return. Mr. President, I'd have to say, I'm the daughter of an extraordinary man, whose inner limpidity has never been muddied by opacity from the outside, which is the reason he isn't presiding or vice-presiding over anything, and spends his time studying and writing, on his little veranda, or he looks after my mother who, in turn, lovingly looks after him. My brothers and I love him, we see to all of his needs, and our mother's as well. We need a model of empathy: that word, currently fashionable, and therefore lackluster, is an elixir against the world's ferocity, difficult though it may be to find it uncorrupted by fictions. The model is my father, empathic to the highest degree. Our lives, as his children, still amount to a desperate attempt to resemble him, or at least to not do anything, at least now that he's an old man, to cause him grief.

But I've understood that it's a minefield, these courteous rejections of my father; my exposition wouldn't work. I, to my misfortune, am not like him; his ability to push against evil is equal to his capacity to understand it. In me it's mutated into an extreme political intransigence that won't let anyone off the hook, and that distresses me, above all. The risk, therefore, if I really am able to speak with the president, is that in order not to wrong my father, a man who's left the scene and relinquished his power, I'd end up being rude to an elderly person who has never left the scene, and today holds the highest office of the land. So, I'm better off preparing a clear-cut CV of Pietro Vella for Luisa, hoping it ends up being seen by the honest eyes of a few members of the commission, or even lands on the president's desk. Then we'll see. If my father doesn't make the cut in the end, they'll have me to contend with.

3.

I prepared the CV and attached it to the email to Luisa. Then, as it turned out, I had a great deal of work, and that work gave me such a headache that I stopped dealing not only with the matter of the list, but I also didn't pay attention to my daughters, nor to the man with whom I've been in a complicated relationship for the past few years.

He's the same person I mentioned as my source regarding the list of twenty-eight. The last time we saw each other, he said, with a sarcasm I didn't appreciate: your illustrious father has been put on the list, but illustriousness goes to waste, there are no longer twenty-eight teachers but fifty. I wasn't surprised: I knew the nominees would have grown in number, that the list would be increasingly packed with people without any merits, and that in the end, in order to avoid conflict among small but powerful people, they would have summoned a sizable number of lowly employees, without any spark to them, in some big room in the Quirinale, and that they would give a little commemorative medal to all of them. But I got angry instead. I wanted that initiative to retain a certain dignity, I wanted my father to be truly celebrated, with great pomp. So, for starters, I got upset, mocking Silvio, that's how I'll call my friend. The desire to spend time with him vanished in an instant, even though we hadn't seen each other in a while, and I'd really wanted things to go well. "Your illustrious father," "illustriousness goes to waste," how dare he? I already struggled, on the whole, to relax and enjoy myself; but then, if something raises my hackles, I can't stand even a caress.

—Trying to be funny? I asked him.

—Not at all.

—Then don't you dare talk that way about my father anymore.

—What did I say?

—Forget about it.

I got dressed, and even though he tried to hold me back with sweet gestures and rough ones—he grabbed hold of my wrist and hissed: if you go out that door, you'll never see me again—I left.

When I was outside, I started crying. I couldn't calm down. I didn't cry for him, who was, on the whole, a patient man, the most patient I've come across, but because I was exhausted, which, on top of feeling dazed, on top of having a stomachache and a backache, was drilling a hole in my chest. I don't cut corners with myself, not at work nor with anything else; I'm incapable of keeping one foot in and one foot out, setting limits to my involvement. I probably ended up with a body not able to take on the tasks I put myself up to, and one of these days I'll collapse on the street, they'll push me to the edges of a dumpster overflowing with other trash that the seagulls rummage through with their beaks. But this is a country whose constant refrain is: it's not my fault. Nothing is said and done as it should be, and I end up feeling like I'm playing the part of the whip of cords that Jesus grasped when he chased the merchants out of the temple. I fight hard, I do, and I don't let up. Nevertheless, on days like this, when I can't go on, what strikes me and scares me is that I'd like to grab a sharp knife, not to make a clean sweep of the temple, or any other institution that thinks it can have its way, but to cut myself, with precision, all over my body.

During this intensely stressful phase of work, I sent my daughters to my parents' house, and for a few days all I did was deal with various troubles. Silvio called often, but I didn't pick up, not because I bore a grudge, simply because I was worn out. Instead I replied to my mother, I said: okay, I'll pop over to your place, but I'll leave the girls there another few days. The fact that my daughters are often at their grandparents' calms me down; if I were their age again, and could go back to live in that house, I'd feel better. I left when I was eighteen, I got married at twenty-two, but I did that because of my yearning for life. I'm not like those that hate their original families, and their own childhoods and teenaged years. I adore my mother, and I hope I've made it clear how much I love my father. It's this life of ongoing struggle that's getting increasingly harder to bear.

This is what I told my mother. I tossed off, when she seemed worried that I looked pale and worn-down: I'm happy here, it's out there that I feel bad. Then I went to the girls to say good-bye (the older one is fourteen, the second twelve, the next eight, and the youngest five: I'm harebrained, why on earth did I have four children?). My mother stayed in the kitchen. Naturally, they were with my father. I walked down the hallway, and I heard his voice, lovely, unveiled. I stopped; the study door was open. He was sitting on an old armchair, and I saw him in pro-file. He had the little one on his knee, and his other three grand-children were sitting on colored pillows spread out on the floor. It was a scene I'd witnessed a hundred times. He was telling them something, or maybe not telling, maybe explaining is the right world. He did the same thing with me, with Sergio, with Ernesto, and whether it was a mechanical device, or a work of art, or the unfolding of a battle, it makes no difference. He was explaining something, and it was as if, in the space between himself and the girls, he were unfurling an old map with inscriptions and colored figures and detailed landscapes. My daughters looked at him, silently, and I liked, above all, the way that Nadina, the oldest, was gazing at him. The marked but nevertheless beautiful face of her grandfather blinded her. I said to myself: I was like that, and I'd still like to be like that, what a pity to have deprived myself of all that, too soon. I leaned my shoulder against the hallway wall and predicted the chorus of protests that would greet me were I to burst into the veranda, like an inevitably chill wind. I imagined the older two with an irritated grimace, the third who would have most likely turned quickly around, hissing: go away, mamma, and the little one woefully torn between her grandfather and me. I returned to the kitchen on the tips of my toes. My mother said:

—He never leaves them be.

—They don't want to be left alone.

—Maybe.

—Furthermore, if he enchants them, you don't need to work as hard.

—It takes a lot of energy to enchant them, and your father gets tired.

—I don't think so, you think he's tired?

—A little, but that's how he is: if he didn't enchant them, he'd wear himself out even more.

Just then, my cell phone rang, it was Silvio again. I stepped out onto the balcony.

—What is it?

—You still angry?

—No.

—Then why don't you pick up?

—I'm afraid.

—Of what?

—Of everything. I'm afraid everything is falling apart.

—The two of us?

—I said everything, not the two of us.

—I have some nice news for you.

—Let's hear it.

—There's some guy on the commission who's crazy about your father.

—One with pull?

—Seems so, I checked out Wikipedia, and he's done a ton of things.

—What's his name?

—Franco Gilara. Know him?

I said no but I wasn't sure. When I got off the call, I went back to the kitchen with that name in my head. I asked my mother:

—Does the name Franco Gilara ring a bell?

She looked at me with slight unease.

—You really don't remember Franco Gilara?

—No.

—Emma, it's Franchino.

4.

We spoke for a bit about this Franchino. Little by little I started to recall that he was one of the many people who would come to our house three or four decades ago, people who were, for the most part, involved with education. My mother asked, studying me with her eyes, if the reason I was asking about Franco Gilara had something to do with work. I was uncertain what to reveal for a moment, but in the end, I decided to tell her about the day dedicated to education, without going into details, however, but merely as something on the horizon. She turned morose, and when her mood darkens, she hunches, like a flower with its corolla bent down.

—If it's still up in the air, don't say anything to your father.

—I'm not planning on talking to him about it.

—You know how he is, good news excites him right away, but then, if nothing happens, he gets upset.

—But how's his relationship with Franchino?

—There is no relationship.

—Why?

She furrowed her brow and shook her head slightly, sighing.

—Your father is a magnet. You end up attached to him and you don't even know how it happened. From then on, you need him, one hundred percent, but he keeps you hanging on along with a thousand other people. If you don't want to get hurt, you have to detach yourself, purposefully.

—What do you mean?

—Franchino, at a certain point, told him it was best if they didn't see each other anymore.

—So they have a terrible relationship?

—Of course not. Dad doesn't have a terrible relationship with anyone, even with the people he can't stand.

—And Franchino?

—I don't think Franchino is mad at him: when someone grows fond of him, that doesn't go away.

As she spoke, another one of our conversations came to mind, from many years ago. I was twenty-six years old, married, and didn't have kids at the time. I'd gone to France for work, to a party, in a castle decked out in a way I'd never seen. I'd had a fair amount to drink, and I latched onto someone who worked for an important newspaper, unlike me in those days, when I slaved away at a meager publication. The guy was my age, I'd known him for a long time. He made me laugh all night, I drank and laughed, and for the first time, I cheated on my husband. And it was amazing, really amazing, but not the sex, I care next to nothing about sex. I remember, instead, the swelling of proportions that followed. I walked down tree-lined avenues at seven in the morning, the air was lovely, and I felt I'd grown as tall as a giant. But then that sense of swelling proportions dissolved, and I started to feel terrible. Not about my husband, honestly, I didn't feel the least bit guilty. In any case, I believed I had the right to enjoy life. Rather, I was afraid of going to my parents' house, and I was certain that my father would have said, right away: Emma, what's happened, without a question mark. He has those blue eyes that see things without questioning, calmly, so much more than others see, and you end up telling him every detail, because all you have to do is talk to him and you feel better, he emanates a fluid energy that's reassuring. So, no big deal, I knew that he would have understood anyway, the way he always understands, and that he would have given me a hug. The problem, rather, was that I felt ashamed, not of what I'd done, but of having to tell him about it. And so I avoided every potential get-together with him and my mother, until the remnants of that night of the party had completely faded from my mind. And even then, I avoided my father, I mainly talked to my mother. That was when I asked her, point-blank: did you ever cheat on Dad? She stared at me for a long time, as if the question were gravely offensive, and she replied with a few words that made no sense: your father is so absolutely indispensable to me that, in order to be able to stay with him, I had to betray him many times, within all the possible and acceptable definitions of "betrayal." The words were uttered without irony, even that phrase, which made no sense—acceptable definitions of betrayal—and with a pain that I never imagined she was capable of feeling. She's always been an energetic woman, with an inner light that keeps darkness at a distance, even when it's pitch-black. I said nothing more, and I beat a hasty retreat, as if I'd seen a snake.

But now that reply from over twenty years ago revisited me, and I asked:

—So, in your opinion, if I ask Franchino to support Dad's candidacy, will he do it?

She seemed concerned at the idea that I was going to get in touch with Franchino. She said:

—It's useless for you to talk to Franchino. He'll always support him, in any case. But in my opinion, it's better to let things be, your father's fine as he is. He studies and writes for hours every day, now and then people come by to visit him, he and I have long conversations on a variety of topics. Just think, he's started studying math for the umpteenth time, without understanding a thing about it. And then you've seen him with the girls, they adore him. What does he need this recognition for?

I didn't reply. I heard my father and my daughters in the hallway. All five of them appeared in the kitchen, surprised to find me there, and we had a lovely evening. While he entertained us, all of us females, making sure to neglect nobody, from the youngest to the eldest, I thought—I believe for the first time in my life—even if my mother did something behind his back, he most surely hasn't been faithful to her. He must have betrayed her discreetly, maybe even chastely, but constantly. And on the whole, I thought it was wonderful that these two old people whom I loved, in order to live together all their lives, had to come up with an innocent way of cheating on one another that enabled them to never say: let's break up.

I had never been capable of adjusting the reality of facts to my advantage, and maybe that's why I was so exhausted. As I returned to my place, I thought, maybe that small prize for my father meant more to me than to him. Given that nothing in my life added up, I was insisting on a recognition for a person I loved, one who managed to make everything add up.

5.

I gradually emerged from that tunnel of professional tension, anxiety, clashes, and threats. That's why, when Silvio found a way to put me in contact with Franco Gilara, I called him and met him in the neighborhood of Piazza Colonna. When I saw him he seemed much older than my father, even though I now knew that he was five years younger, my mother's age. There was no aspect of him that I remembered: he was short, overweight, broad-shouldered, with a huge neck that bore the whitish folds of his face, descending from his very thin lips. He, on the other hand, recognized me right away—or pretended to, and his eyes lit up, he exclaimed: Emma, you are your mother's twin, and concluded devotedly under his breath, devotedly: a beautiful woman. It's something I hear often, and it always bothers me a bit, as if, due to an oversight, I'd lost out on the opportunity to look like my father. We stepped into a café. He was in a hurry, in spite of his age he was a man with a clogged schedule, with thousands of things to do. He immediately said:

—You don't need to ask me a thing, it's all set.

—What?

—Your father's one of the three, and the other two don't make him look at all bad, they're distinguished people.

He told me their names. It was true, and I was satisfied. But at that point, he went on to ask me if I was absolutely sure—as Luisa had told him—that Teresa Quadraro would take part in the ceremony. He belabored that point:

—Listen up, Emma, the president is really invested in this.

—She'll be there, trust me.

—I'm saying this precisely because I trust you. I've been following your career from the start, and I know perfectly well that you do things the right way.

—This isn't work for me, it's an homage to my father. I'm positive that Professor Quadraro will be delighted to speak at the ceremony.

—People say that she doesn't have the greatest personality, on the contrary, let's just say that they call her an old hag ready to denigrate everyone—and, in particular, all things Italian.

—She must have her reasons.

—Do you know how to track her down?

—I'll figure it out, don't worry.

—Tell her that the president wants to meet with her privately.

—I believe the one getting the prize is the teacher, not the student.

—Of course. You're good with words, very good. You got that from your father, not your mother.

—My father can't be beat.

Franchino was staring at my hand on the table. He seemed upset by the color of my nail polish.

—Indeed, no one can beat him. The first time I heard him speaking in public, I thought he was saying a boatload of trivial things, but he said them well, so well that I struggled to stick to my position. And on a second public occasion, I criticized him, point by point, I hated his books. But then he talked to me in that way he has, you know what I mean, in that authentic way, that's so reassuring, and I felt, more and more, the need to remain by his side.

—It happens to everyone.

He nodded yes, he took a deep breath, he had to go. He got up with a bit of an effort after leaving a tip on the table that was twice the amount of what we'd consumed. I also got up. As we stepped out of the café, he dried the saliva in the corner of his mouth with the back of his finger, kissed me on the cheeks, and repeated:

—Remember, Emma, I'm putting my trust in you.

—You, sir, need to trust my father above all: he'll shine a light on the entire Italian school system. In the very end, it's really the story of your friendship that should reassure you. You had a bad opinion about what he wrote, and then you had to change your mind.

—Bravissima, that's exactly right. But you're incredibly smart, and I want to say goodbye leaving you with a jumbled thought that I can't unravel, so much so that, if you can, and if you send me an email with a clearer way of putting it, I'd be happy: I changed my mind, while still thinking I was right. Ciao, bella.

I shouted out behind him:

—Well then, why did you fight to get him into the list of three?

Once more he waved to me with his hand, without turning back, and slipped around the corner.

Now I'm angry again. I added up the old, unintentionally cryptic words of my mother and the intentionally incongruous words of Franchino. It was as if they'd consulted one another over the decades and both arrived at the conclusion that the only way to talk about their relationships with my father was to formulate an illogical proposition. At this point I felt like laughing because, perhaps feeling influenced, I also thought of a similar sentence. Just wait, I said to myself: I'm so used to always being a problem that in this little venture, one that's all my own, I'm in danger of turning into a problem for myself.

6.

I never got hold of Teresa Quadraro's number, but I got her email right away, and I wrote to her in detail about Pietro, the honor, and the importance of her saying something at the ceremony. I did so with all the courtesy I could muster, tossing out, here and there, that my father spoke of her often, with affection and enormous admiration. In fact, I don't recall a single time that my father mentioned her name. He's a man who never brags about anything, not even his close friendships. My mother, meanwhile, every time Quadraro would show up on television, would say: see that woman, she owes it all to Papà, she was his student.

I hoped I hadn't written anything that might have put her off, and I clicked send. I figured I'd have to wait days, maybe weeks. I had factored in the need for a reminder, the need for pressing words as opposed to bland ones, even recourse to the president. Instead, after exactly twelve minutes, Teresa Quadraro replied. Just a few lines, but incisive ones: Dear Emma, I've heard your name for decades. Your father often spoke and wrote to me about you. I'm pleased that you've thought of me for this lovely occasion. I'd be delighted to speak at the ceremony in your father's honor. Let me know that date. Nothing more, that was the gist of what she wrote.

I forwarded the professor's email to Franchino, I told him to reassure the president, everything was set. Then I set off straightway for my parents' house to tell them the news. Amelia, the woman who keeps house for them, answered the buzzer. My mother was out looking for presents for Nadina, which was why I suddenly remembered that her birthday was coming in a few days. I went up anyway to talk to my father. Amelia indicated that he was on the veranda, as usual.

That's where I went, but he wasn't there. I was about to return to the kitchen when I looked through the glass. He was on the little terrace, leaning over with his elbows on the railing, but in an awkward position, looking not down but up, maybe at a seagull, or at the pigeons. I called out: Papà! He turned around abruptly. He stood up straight, with a pained look on his face, and said:

—I'm so pleased to see you, you looked tired the other day. Come here, give me a kiss.

I kissed him.

—I have some lovely news to give you.

—Let's hear it.

—You're getting a prize.

—Who's giving it to me?

—The president of the Republic. They're giving you a prize along with two other teachers, for all the things you've written and done for the school system.

—That was a long time ago.

—Thank goodness memory nourishes good things.

—Yes, thank goodness.

—What's wrong? What is it, are you sad?

—I'm pleased as can be. It's just that you seem a little stirred up, and I'm sorry.

—I'm not stirred up because I'm worried, but because I'm happy. And that's not all, the president wanted one of your students to be at the ceremony, to say nice things about you.

—Did they find someone?

—They've all queued up, Papà, and you know it. But I found the best one.

—What do you mean?

—I got in touch with your most illustrious pupil, and she said she'll be there.

Something now happened that upset me. Something darted though my father's blue eyes: not amazement, not worry, but a viscous flicker of fear and rage that landed squarely in my chest.

—Who is she? he asked, his voice curdling.

I have never heard such violence reverberating from him, never, not even when I was a teenager and my mother forced him to reproach me. The joy vanished in an instant, and I murmured, with tears that already wanted to gush from my eyes, streaming like blood:

—Teresa Quadraro.

THE THIRD STORY

1.

I don't like the way the daughter writes, or the father. I pre-
fer sentences that don't force themselves to sound pretty
to convey behaviors and states of mind. But both of them
tend to do this, and they disturb me. Emma is convinced that
she's got great literary talent, like most people who write for
newspapers, and she tries to prove this above all to herself,
even when she writes an email. Pietro, on the other hand, is
surprising, as usual. In the past, even though he's revealed a
great passion for literature, he's never mentioned that he's had
ambitions to be a writer. Even his letters were always lists of
facts, each summarized in a few words, often self-mocking
ones. But now, after almost twenty-five years of silence, he
sends me a huge attachment in which, from page one, he aims
to transform himself into a literary being. No one ages grace-
fully, and he hasn't, either, in spite of having a great capacity
for self-control. The text might have been bearable had it been
brief, and above all, had he stuck to that economical way of
writing he taught me when I was his student, which he himself
had employed. But he wasn't able to hold back and, now that
he's nearing eighty, he's written the novel about his life, naturally with great claims of truthfulness, even though, from the
very beginning—and he taught me this—telling a story means
lying, and the better the liar, the better the storyteller.

Nothing unforgivable, in any case, apart from perhaps the
length. Two hundred and thirty pages, that's too much. I read
a hundred, and it was enough for me, especially because,

immediately afterward, he starts to tell the story, in great detail, of his troubled experience as a politician immune to corruption, which I find incredibly boring. Emma, too, in her email, struggles to get to the point. She likes to say, over and over, that she's the champion of all things good and just in a country where the good and the just amount to nothing. She enjoys presenting herself as someone so powerful that she's even got an in with the president of the Republic, that is to say, with a man she places on the ladder well below her father. But all you need to do is read between the lines to realize that she's still a child terrified of being reproached by adults, and that makes you like her. Pietro, meanwhile, can't be boiled down to likeability. Rather, his text contains extremely unlikeable elements. I don't think it's nice, for example, that he's painted me as undisciplined rabble-rouser. If I were what he says I am, I wouldn't be here, now, a few steps from Washington Square, but in the small town I grew up in. And his daughter wouldn't have written to me, giving it all she's got, to convince me.

But that's not all. I thought it was childish that he attributed the invention of the growl game to himself—our playful reduction of all the arts and sciences to an argh, an ugh, an ooh ooh ooh. That's my thing, one of the few things from those days I still care about. Instead, I was disturbed by that way he described our meeting in Milan. In that instance, and I don't know why, he put the contrivance of ethical marriage into my mouth. He, not I, was the one who gave that name to our bond, and who kept writing to me, obsessively, and keeping me abreast of all that he did. That I often wrote back is also a falsehood. My whole life, I probably sent him ten letters at the most.

But it's useless to call him on it: That phase ended a while back, nor am I the kind of person who responds to another person's pulp novel with my own. If, however, my brain should soften to the point of summoning me to scribble one down, it would be extremely short. I was born in Rome, on a pretty little street in a hamlet outside the city called La Rustica, and today I live in Manhattan. I had an intense life, and an extremely fortunate one. I've lived on no less than four continents. I've benefited from gradual but ongoing success in my job. I've met very smart people, with whom I've had very smart conversations, braiding together very smart bonds. But Pietro Vella, my teacher at a high school on the outskirts, was the only man I've loved, and love still.

2.

Once you lift away the niceties, the kernel of Emma's letter is that the Italian nation wants to bestow an honor on Pietro, but it necessitates my going to Rome to say good things about his work as a teacher. I'm a woman who is almost seventy-two years old, with various aches and pains that I manage to keep under control in this challenging city only thanks to my economic means and my many connections, given that I'm a well-known figure. Every morning I walk under the Arch, cross Washington Square, and order a cappuccino in a coffee shop just a few feet from the monument dedicated to Fiorello La Guardia, where there's a young Albanian who can make a good coffee. Twice I week, I head to Citarella on Sixth Avenue, where I buy fish, challah, and orange juice. In the winter I like the bare trees, the fountain drained of water that serves as a stage for daring jugglers, the moment the lampposts shine with light. In spring I study the branches that turn green, the arrival of the first flowers, and now and then, I leaf through the *New York Times* on one of the benches, sitting in the sun, crowded with the elderly who, like me, have fragile and frozen bones. Until a few years ago, I used to walk gladly through the park, among the waves of tourists, male and female students in purple caps and gowns, and disoriented parents who come from who knows which America for their child's graduation. These days, after having broken my femur, I've had to undergo a long and very costly rehabilitation, so I don't walk much. Generally, I'll walk on a Sunday afternoon. I listen to the saxophone player's music under Garibaldi's statue. I often argue with the kids who show off on their skateboards and threaten to knock me down. I circle around the young pianist who invites tourists to lie down under his piano, which has a sign on one side that says: *This machine kills fascists*, something that, unfortunately, was untrue even when Woody Guthrie was around. It's only when I feel really alone that I go to the theater with some friends, or go out to dinner, in one of the few restaurants where the customers aren't screaming, with older gentlemen who safeguard me as if I were a relic.

These are the habits that help with old age. Italy, as I make clear, isn't a part of them. There's no Rome, no countryside left in the hamlet where I was born. Those are twilight places, at once extremely sharp in my mind and also blurry. At dawn, until I'm fully awake, I move through them with ease, but I'm not able to place them in any real geography. Only one place is rigorously specific: the classroom my third year of high school, the first on the right, just after the staircase. Pietro came in one morning, he put his cloth bag stuffed with books on the lectern. I think he was twenty-five years old, maybe less. From that moment, I did everything so that he'd notice me, and he did everything to ignore me. For three years, my afternoons, nights, Sundays, ordained holidays, and summer vacations were clear indicators of what death was like. I only felt alive at school, and he appeared punctually in the classroom, and the whole world rebooted. He'd sit down, stand up, lean against the wall, go over to the window. His fingers would brush the chalk, the blackboard, the desks, while his voice injected power into the name of each person, place, and thing, every verb, adverb, and adjective. He never touched us, not even in the course of a friendly gesture, or a handshake for appearance's sake, or an arm around the shoulders. And yet he touched us, intimately, with his words. I, in particular, felt so shamelessly frisked that I'd leave school exhausted.

One time, a student in another one of his classes, older than we were, got really angry, and we heard him cursing at him in the hallway. After that, I walked home on purpose with that boy. He wasn't able to calm himself down, mainly because he wasn't able to articulate, in words, what had so infuriated him. He only kept saying: it's crushing, it's too much, and what he meant was both that Pietro's lessons were so dense that, in the end, there was too much to study, and also that our prof emanated some kind of fluid energy, which rendered him unbearable, precisely as a teacher. Both things were likely true. You had to study a lot with him, too much, and what's more, his person tailed us even after he said goodbye to us with a nod, left the classroom, and abandoned us to ourselves. The crushing aspect, in other words, was real, and I—like all the others, and also like that student—worked hard to evade him, and nevertheless, longed to be crushed.

From the first day of school, I started to battle with him. I gave it all I had because, in order to be defeated, I wanted him to give his all, too. I interrupted his lectures, I posed questions, I made fun of his replies. It was useless, Pietro never batted an eye. Every provocation was, for him, an excuse to be more exact. And that's just how he was, he gave the best of himself whenever I gave him trouble. It was a blinding spectacle to see and feel how his body, his mind, would search for and locate the proper measure, the one specific to me. Back then, I hadn't seen other teachers who operated that way, causing rack and ruin and affection. I was alarmed, but what else is a good teacher supposed to do? If I don't pine for Italy, I certainly pine for the three years when, on the outskirts of Rome, Pietro was my literature teacher. And so, given this sentiment, I immediately replied to Emma: ok, I'll make this extremely boring trip, I'll do it for your father. But I'd just sent the email when I remembered another place: the long road that led from the piazza to the high school that I traversed each morning on foot, among the low buildings and across the fields full of dilapidated huts, gray brick sheds, debris glinting in the weeds.

I saw myself on that road. It's November, it's cold, and it's raining. A car slows to a crawl, the window is rolled down, and I recognize the new teacher who makes me tremble, even just to look at him. All he says is, Get in. I look at him and I'm scared. I reply, almost angry, No. He blinks his long dark lashes, he seems scared of the fear he's perceived in my face. He proceeds without saying anything else, and I stare at the hatchback that drives away. Something broke for a second, inside and outside of me.

3.

Emma has written me another long email. She says that the organizational team has already defined a great number of details, and that they'll see to my every wish. Then she proceeds in stops and starts, with studied remarks. The father's delighted that I've accepted, he's spoken to her at length about what a wonderful student I was. Whereas he said nothing about the fact that we were involved. It was her mother who told her that, just yesterday, which she transcribes for me, making light of it. Nadia told her: yes, she wasn't just his best pupil, but something more. School wasn't the only thing she was good at, apparently. At this point she launches into a detailed story about her troubled relationships with men. The aim is to link her unhappy affairs to mine with her father. I wasn't lucky, she says, neither my husband nor my lovers ever turned into friends, the rancor prevailed. She hopes, instead, that I remember Pietro with fondness, and then she goes on to praise him for another twenty lines, as a teacher, as an intellectual, as a man—she practically wants to craft the speech that I'll be giving. She signs off reassuring me that she can't wait to meet me.

This email got on my nerves. At first it occurred to me that both the father's pulp novel and the daughter's invitation might be part of the same strategy, orchestrated by Pietro himself, to end our affair with a big splash. But now I realize that it was Emma who put this whole contraption in place, without consulting her parents beforehand. All you need to do is read between the lines to realize that Nadia isn't happy about digging me up again, and that Pietro, as usual, is worried about how I'll behave. So then why on earth am I going to Rome?

I went out for a walk to calm down, even though this month of May is antagonistic toward the elderly: one day it's warm, the next day it's freezing. Tonight it's tepid. It's still light out, but the lampposts are blazing. I stopped to chat with the drug dealers that hang out by the chess tables. I walked along the avenues, breathing in the aroma of flowers and hashish. I reached the fountain that shoots out high white streams, where the kids love getting wet, where young girls pose seductively in the spray while a band plays music. I went to see the black man who eats, drinks, and makes paintings in the style of Pollock, and sleeps on a hot slab of metal next to one of the university entrances. But I didn't feel better.

Fifty years have gone by, and I'm preparing to go to Rome to meet Pietro the way I did when, after I graduated from high school, I went to wait for him at the school with the intention of telling him verbatim: I loved you for three years and now I want to be loved back. That's just how I said it, using the friendly "tu" even though we'd addressed each other with the formal "lei" up until then. There's more: I kissed him on the lips. It was an instant, it was like a blow, and he raised his left hand, as if to protect himself.

We were in a café steps from the school, we'd ordered something, I forget, and we'd talked about my plans for future study. Pietro paid, we headed for the exit, I uttered those words to him, and I gave him that kiss. Who knows what I was expecting, over fifty years ago. Everything he did and said was an excessive promise. But the young man who seduced us all with the many things that he knew, with the emphasis he put into each word, placed, between us and him, a polite distance we could never overcome, but that each of us would have wanted to overcome. Now I'd overcome that distance, and I demanded that he give not what he'd already given me in the classroom, but what no one other than me, in that moment, might receive. Perhaps he realized it just before I declared my love for him, just before I kissed him. I wanted more, more, not sex but the hyperuranian ideal to which, I believe, he must have attributed the person who showed up each day in the classroom. Except that either that ideal didn't exist, or he hid it from me from the very start, and went on to dazzle other young girls, as if I weren't enough for him.

I've never met a man in my life who was so submissively available to feminine yearning. Those were times when proclaiming, to the world, that you were really free overlapped with open sexual availability. He cheated on me, and I cheated on him more than he did, in plain sight. We humiliated each other and extolled each other, reciprocally. But in the three years that we were together, the many joys were always less joyous than I expected, and the many sorrows were ignored or quickly chalked up to the catalogue of paltry grievances of the petty bourgeoisie. I don't know how many times we broke up with loathing, and then seized each other again, with ferocious zeal. Until I proposed that experiment: let's reveal the worst of ourselves to one another, far, far worse than what we've already revealed. Naturally, when I made that proposal, I already knew I'd leave him, I couldn't take it anymore. We do so many stupid things when we're young. No trace should remain of youth, not even a memory. Pietro, on the other hand, wanted to leave traces, given all that he wrote. In that so-called novel of his, he tends to hide the fact that, from a certain point forward, and especially with the advent of email, he started to treat writing like a strait-jacket. I've never met a man so full of life, and more afraid of his own bewitching fullness. He exaggerated, he overflowed, and he used me to hold himself back. He acted as if he were sure that the two of us, together but apart, could keep each other in check. But it wasn't a solid conviction, he's never had any conviction that was solid. One time, talking about his job, he wrote to me, desolate: no matter how much you study, how many titles you earn, it's easy to be Hyde, harder to become Jekyll.

4.

In the end, I go to Rome. If, in New York, there was a mix of hot and cold, here it's just cold. But the city's just as dirty, and I don't feel safe here, either; with each step I take, I'm afraid of tripping, and ending up in some hospital with a broken bone. I got rid of Emma a few minutes ago. To her misfortune, she looks like her mother, not her father. This woman didn't get anything from Pietro, only the upbringing he gave her. While we were talking, I thought: In some sense, we're both his pupils; if we examined ourselves carefully, who knows how many fragments of knowledge, how many expressions we'd discover in common.

In any case, one difference is quite clear: Emma is almost always out of line. What torments her now is what I'll be saying tomorrow. I tried, for a long time, to avoid confessing that

I didn't know, but then, when she asked if she could have a copy of my speech, with the excuse of wanting to publish in it the paper she worked for, I told her that not only was there no text, but not even an outline. I'd be improvising on the spot.

This deeply upset her, and I believe she struggled to refrain from making one of the scenes she must be used to making. Disappointed, she came close to confessing the truth to me. She said: my father's gotten quite worked up, and knowing what you're going to say would calm him down. Her father, her father, that's all she talks about. Is it possible that everyone loved that man to death, even the children, who always cultivate some hate, or rather, repugnance, toward their parents? I told her: after all these years, your father should trust me. It was just what she wanted to hear. She cheered up, it almost looked like she was moved, and she exclaimed: I'll call him on the cell phone, can you tell him that? I said no, we'll speak tomorrow.

I went to bed and thought back to those things we'd said in confidence so many years ago. I'll tell him, at the end of the day: the experiment is a success, life's over, we're safe. And I'll add, to make fun of him, it's not the pedagogy of love that improves us, but the pedagogy of fear.

I turned this last sentence around in my head. We feared that our terrible deeds would haunt us and lord over us forever. And yet, today, I barely remember what I told him I'd done, and I'm surprised that I recall little of what he'd confided in me. Surely, they were dreadful things, but not dreadful enough to be unforgettable, and I went on to see and hear others that were much worse. Maybe it might even be a nice thing, tomorrow, after the ceremony, to see each other somewhere, and talk about how rotten we used to feel back then.

The idea appealed to me for a while, but then I thought back to some of Pietro's extremely exceptional moments, brief flashes of memory that I've pushed back over the years. They

weren't images of our quarrels, even though on some occasions
they veered closed to getting violent. They were moments that
seemed lovely, he with his face concentrated, his mouth half
open, his eyes fixed on something invisible while he ruffled his
hair with his fingers. Until I noticed that something truly repel-
lent was coursing through his entire being, like an unbearable
spasm of the nervous system. I would immediately retract my
gaze, horrified. But not him, he continued to stay on the alert,
as if he were seeing himself. At times I asked him, Pietro,
what's wrong? He'd explain it to me willingly, also self-mock-
ingly. It's the malady of my origins, he'd say. I'm the first of six
siblings, the family was poor, my father was an electrician and
my mother was a housewife; it's the malady of not being capable enough, from elementary school until I received my university degree I never felt worthy; it's the malady of the degra-
dation of roles, I know I'm a teacher without substance, and
I'm among those who are lowering, in epic proportions, the
quality of intellectual work; it's the malady of a well-propor-
tioned body and harmonious features: beauty gives you a faulty
advantage, it's the most unjust form of getting ahead.

Each time, he'd invent some sociological or ethical reason
for his malady. But at other times he seemed trapped; he wasn't
able to back out of those terrible moments, or even to hear me.
He sat there, observing himself, enabling one malady after
another to spring forth, and even though I called out to him, I
couldn't distract him.

I loved him deeply, and I'd wanted to save him, but there
was no redeeming him. In that moment, I was terrified by the
cruelty of his forehead, by the upper lip that curled ferociously,
as if he had a twitch, by the way his face contorted, and I'd
have to go. No, I really don't know what I'll say tomorrow.
Pietro was, and is, a very dangerous man.

5.

Things aren't going as they should. Emma arrived right on time, as did Nadia. I'd never seen her apart from once, from far away, back when I was still jealous. I'd thought she was gorgeous, and it had made me suffer. Now, with a certain satisfaction, I saw that she was overweight, and that she'd aged badly, even though she surely has fewer ailments than I do. I pretended not to notice that she was quite disgruntled and intimidated. It's natural: I'm the center of attention, the president treated me like a monument that deserves a laurel crown, and I've influenced the lives of countless people, her husband's above all; she's a retired high school teacher, she lived pent up, begrudgingly, in her own dejection and, above all, was never able to govern the man she loved, not even a little bit.

—Pietro—she said—sent me away so that he could practice his thank you speech in peace.

It's old age—I replied—I've never seen Pietro at a loss for words.

Mother and, above all, daughter did not appreciate that display of familiarity, and maybe I didn't appreciate it myself, either. We always end up showing a bit of the worst of us, buried deep down.

An hour has gone by, and Pietro hasn't turned up. The two women, now one, now the other, have started calling him at brief intervals, but he hasn't picked up once. Nadia said: I hope he hasn't decided not to come at the last minute. He hates this government; he watches the politicians on TV and says: I might have taught this riffraff. I couldn't hold back a chuckle, and said, if he picks up, I'll talk to him. There was a flicker of anger in her eyes, and she murmured, as if speaking to herself: I'll go home and drag him here by force, and then she headed toward the exit, tailed by a few people who were asking: has the *professore* arrived? Before following her mother, Emma, who had turned extremely pale, told me: you and Papà should have worked out your problems beforehand. Again, I felt like laughing—on certain occasions all I do is laugh, it's a laughter of intolerance that seeps into my words, even when there's nothing to laugh at—and I replied: we resolved all that there was to resolve long before you were born.

Now I'm here, seated in the front row, next to the frowning president. It's obvious that Pietro isn't turning up, and that I'll never see him again. What a pity. I finally knew what I'd say, and in this sickly-hued hall, in the presence of my former teacher, I'd have gladly spoken. I was, and am, far more dangerous than he.

T o write, first and foremost, is to choose the words to tell a story, whereas to translate is to evaluate, acutely, each word an author chooses. Repetitions in particular rise instantly to the surface, and they give the translator particular pause when there is more than one way to translate a particular word. On the one hand, why not repeat a word the author has deliberately repeated? On the other hand, was the repetition deliberate? Regardless of the author's intentions, the translator's other ear, in the other language, opens the floodgates to other solutions.

The Italian word that caught my ear above all others in this novel was *invece*. It appears three times in the volcanic first paragraph and occurs a total of sixty-four times from beginning to end. *Invece*, which pops up constantly in Italian conversation, was a familiar word to me. It means "instead" and serves as an umbrella for words like "rather," "on the contrary," "on the other hand," "however," "meanwhile," and "in fact." A compound of the preposition *in* and the noun *vece*—the latter means "place" or "stead"—it derives from the Latin *invicem*, which in turn is a compound of *in* and the noun *vicis*, declined as *vice* in the ablative case. When, after completing a first draft of my translation of *Trust*, I looked up *vicis* in a few Latin dictionaries, in both Italian and English, I found the following definitions: *change, exchange, interchange, alternation, succession, requital, recompense, retaliation, repayment, place, room, post, office, plight, lot, time, occasion, opportunity, event*, and, in the plural, *danger or risk*.

But let's move forward on the linguistic timeline and back to the Italian term, *invece*, of which Starnone seems either consciously or unwittingly fond. Functioning as an adverb in Italian, it is a word that links one concept to another, that pits one notion against another, that establishes a relationship between different ideas. *Invece* invites one thing to substitute for another, and its robust Latin root gives rise in English to "vice versa" (literally, "the order being changed"), the prefix "vice" (as in the vice president who must stand in for the president if need be), and the word "vicissitude," which means a passing from one state of affairs to the next. After investigating *invece* across three languages, I now believe that this everyday Italian adverb is the metaphorical underpinning of Starnone's novel. For if Starnone's *Ties* (2017) is an act of containment and his *Trick* (2018) an interplay of juxtaposition, *Trust* probes and prioritizes substitution: an operation that not only permeates the novel's arc but describes the process of my bringing it into English. In other words, I believe that *invece*, a trigger for substitution, is a metaphor for translation itself.

Invece insists that circumstances are always changing; without a variation to the norm there is no jagged line of plot, there is only the flat fact of situation. Starnone's penchant for the term reminds us that, essentially, there is no plot of any book, in any language, in which the notion of *invece* is not complicating matters and thus propelling the action forward. It points all the way back to *polytropos*, the epithet Homer uses to describe Odysseus at the start of his epic poem: he is the man of "many twists and turns." To repeat, it is only when one reality or experience or inclination is thrown into question by another that a story gets going.

Fittingly, there is a teeter-totter element running through *Trust*, though a more high-adrenaline diversion, rollercoasters, now comes to mind (*nota bene*: rollercoasters are also referred to as "twisters" in English). Starnone often pauses at

the precise moment in which the rollercoaster, creeping
upward on its trajectory, briefly pauses before hurtling back
down. He emphasizes this moment of drastic transition with
phrases like "*proprio mentre*" or "*proprio quando*"—I translate
them as "just while" or "just when" in Italian. Each time, it sig-
nals a plunge, a lurch, a swoop, a turning upside-down. The
laws of Starnone's fictional universe, which correspond to the
universe in general, remind us that everything in life is always
on the brink of altering, vanishing, or turning on its head. At
times these changes (or rather, vicissitudes) are miraculous and
moving. Other times, they are traumatic and terrifying. In
Starnone's pages, they are always both, and what one appreci-
ates by reading him, and especially by translating him, is just
how skilled he is when it comes to crafting and calibrating fictional time: how nimbly he curves and tilts it, bends and
weaves it, slows it down, speeds it up, enables it to climb and
fall. He builds to breathtaking panoramas and, the next
instant, induces heart-dropping anxiety, primal screams, and
hysterical laughter. Something tells me that Starnone has a hell
of a time laying down these tracks.

Places change, our preferences and predilections change,
people and politics change. Like many of Starnone's novels,
this one toggles between past and present, between Naples and
Rome, between starting out in life and taking stock in old age.
But the most significant reversal is that of roles, between
teacher and student. The student-teacher dynamic is familiar
to most of us, given that most of us have been students at one
time or another. It just so happens that Starnone (and his present translator) has also been on the teaching side of this relationship. It also just so happens that this novel is very much
about the education system: what it means to teach and to be
taught, and why teachers must always learn to teach better.
But what is a teacher, other than a former student whose role
has changed and been replaced by a new one? Where does the

student taper off and the teacher take over? And what happens when a student goes on to learn more than her teacher, and ends up teaching him a thing or two?

This novel recounts a love affair between a male teacher and his former female student: nothing new there, other than the fact that, in light of Me Too, our reading of (and tolerance for) such relationships may have changed. The passage from student to teacher involves a succession, just as the passage from childhood to adulthood, from lover to spouse, from parent to grandparent. No role is ever a fixed role, and this novel traces how one's station in life always wavers as characters shift from obscurity to success, from trying economic circumstances to more comfortable ones. And it traces the vagaries of the human heart, of desire. So much drama is born from the impulse to substitute the person we think we love with another, especially when children are involved.

There is an exchange of words at the heart of this book, words that are never revealed to the reader. This secret exchange of information determines the destinies of two characters—of Pietro Vella, the male protagonist, above all. What is said between the characters (but left unsaid on the page) threatens to overthrow everything—and to introduce chaos, which is always lapping at the shores of everyday mortal reality in Starnone's works. The potential earthquake in *Trust*, at least from Pietro's point of view, regards what a former lover might say about him. Maintaining order (not to mention ensuring that the conventional "plot" of Pietro's life unfolds without incident) depends on not saying things. We can trace a constellation from Dante to Manzoni to Hemingway to Starnone that sheds light on how writers use language to talk about silence and the importance of withholding speech. But the exchange imbedded in the invisible part of the iceberg of *Trust* also carries the threat of retribution, and is a source of peril.

What an intelligent, articulate woman might say has always

been considered dangerous. In Ovid's *Metamorphoses*—a work I happen to be translating as I write these words about Starnone—they have their tongues cut out, or are reduced to echoes, or turn into trees who merely rustle their leaves in acknowledgement, or into animals who low instead of utter sentences. In Ovid, these states of transformation (or mutation) involve a partial or full muting of the female voice, and even mutilation. They may be read both as liberation from—and the consequences of—patriarchal power and predatory behaviors. If we break down the moment of metamorphosis in almost any episode in Ovid, the effect is one of substitution: of body parts being replaced by other animate or inanimate features, one by one. That is to say, hooves appear *instead of* feet, or branches *instead of* arms.[1] This systematic substitution is what allows, in Ovid, for a complete and comprehensive change of form. Not always but often, Ovid walks us through the metamorphosis step by step, slowing things down so that we understand exactly how dynamic and dramatic the process is.

Translation, too, is a dynamic and dramatic transformation. Word for word, sentence for sentence, page for page, until a text conceived and written and read in one language comes to be reconceived, rewritten, and read in another. The translator labors to find alternative solutions, not to cancel out the original, but to counter it with another version. My version of this book was produced to stand in the place of the Italian, so that readers in English might have a relationship with it. It is now an English book instead of—*invece di*—an Italian one.

---

[1] Inspired by my study of *invece* in *Trust*, I am now tracking recurrences of the term *vicis* in *The Metamorphoses*. I'll share, here, two instances in Book Four. In line 40 (the myth of the Minyeides), "*perque vices,*" meaning "by turns," and line 218 (the myth of Clytie and Leucothoe), "*noxque vicem peragit,*" meaning "and night takes her turn." The first instance refers to the alternating trajectory of storytelling; the second, to the turning of time.

Even within a single language, one word can so very often substitute for another. As I said earlier, it is the writer's job, and subsequently the translator's, to choose among them. While the writer typically has one attempt, translation extends this game and complicates it significantly. Given that there are so often multiple terms to say the same thing, we are all playing the substitution game in the way we think, speak, write, and otherwise express ourselves. The dictionary reminds us that there are more synonyms than antonyms. Not all words have an opposite, but the vast majority have stand-ins to augment our understanding, interpretation, and use of them.

Take the Italian word *anzi*, for example, which also appears quite frequently in this novel. It can function as a preposition or an adverb, and it can mean "actually," "on the contrary," "rather," "indeed," and "in fact." In fact, *anzi* can substitute for *invece*, given that if one appends the conjunction *che* to *anzi* ("instead of," "rather than"), it essentially means the same thing as *invece di*. Like *invece*, *anzi* is a syntactical fly in the ointment that draws our attention to a hidden scenario, a hiccup, a twist of fate or mood or point of view. Deriving from the Latin prefix "ante," it posits—in English, too—that time has passed, that things are no longer as they previously were, that a different moment preceded this one, indeed, that you are reading this sentence in this moment as opposed to another.

In this novel there are two terms used for the deepest and potentially most destabilizing emotion we human beings can experience. One is the verb *amare*, which means "to love," and gives us the noun, love (*amore*), that is the novel's first word. *Amore* reinforces the link between *Trust* and Ovid, author not only of the *Ars Amatoria (The Art of Love)* but, of course, of the changing love stories running though the *Metamorphoses*. For the question that drives this book forward is one that anyone who has ever loved has likely reckoned with: What happens when love alters? When it cools, melts, or softens? When it makes room for another? Shakespeare's Sonnet 116 tells us that "Love's not love / Which alters when it alteration finds;" and yet, all the words pertaining to altering and bending in Shakespeare's poem give us pause, and they pave the way for Starnone's steadfast attention to amatory impediments. But in addition to "amare," Starnone pulls the expression *voler bene* into the mix. There is no satisfying English solution for this Italian phrase. Literally, it means to want good things for someone, to wish someone well. But in Italian what it actually means is to feel affection for someone, and thus to love someone, both in a romantic and nonromantic sense. *Amare* and *voler bene* are to some degree interchangeable, and yet they are very distinct. They can have different connotations in different regions of Italy and can suggest one type of love as opposed to another.

An interesting distinction: one can *amare* many things, but one tends to *voler bene* another person (or personified object). *Amare* derives from Latin, as does *voler bene*. Catullus combines these sentiments in poem 72, which begins by comparing his love for Lesbia to a father's fondness for his children. That is to say, the poet's love for her has surpassed the conventional emotional tie between lovers, which is subject to change. The end of the poem reads: "*quod amantem inure talis / cogito amare magis, sed bene velle minus.*" (My English translation would be: "because such harm / drives the lover to love more, but like less," though Francis Warre Cornish's translation reads: "Because such an injury as this / drives a lover to become more of a lover, but less of a friend"[2]). The last line, which has been described as "perfectly balanced,"[3] is poised on the conjunction

[2] The Poems of Gaius Valerius Catullus. Translated by F.W. Cornish, with revisions by C.P. Goold, in *Catullus, Tibullus, Pervigilium Veneris*, Second Edition, revised by G.P Goold. Cambridge, Massachusetts: Harvard University Press, 1988.

[3] *Catullus: The Shorter Poems.* Edited with introduction, translation, and commentary by John Godwin. Warminster, England: Aris & Phillips Ltd, 1999.

sed, meaning "but," which, like *invece*, places two ideas in conversation, the latter modifying the former. In Italian translations, *"velle minus"* turns into *voler bene*, and indicates friendship as opposed to romantic love, or if you will, liking as opposed to loving.[4]

Amare and *voler bene* command our attention in *Trust* from the very beginning; these terms are what we get to know first, and they, along with change, are the real protagonists of Starnone's novel. Think of them as good witch and bad witch; I won't say which witch is which. The degree to which they overlap and challenge each other, the way they correspond with and compete with and cancel one another—much like *invece* and *anzi*—proves that language—or rather, the combination of language and human usage—is impossible to comprehend at face value. We must enter, instead, into a more profound relationship with words—we must descend with them to a deeper realm, uncovering layers of alternatives in a hidden and hermetic realm. The only way to even begin to understand language is to love it so much that we allow it to confound us and to torment us to the extent that it threatens to swallow us whole.

Across the three books, it's been a challenge to substitute Starnone's crisp single-word titles in Italian with a satisfying word in English. Here is the first instance when the original title, *Confidenza*, might have simply been substituted with the English cognate, "Confidence." And yet I chose differently. Like *confidenza*, "confidence" has multiple meanings in English: intimacy, secrecy, and assurance. Starnone's title is bolstered, thematically, by all three meanings. But in Italian *confidenza* points more to the idea of a secret exchange, as

---

[4] *Velle*, an infinitive meaning "to wish or want" in Latin, is just one letter away from Vella, the protagonist's last name. *Vello*, meanwhile, is another Latin verbe that means "I pluck. I pull. I destroy."

opposed to the English sense of trust in one's abilities, or cer-
titude. My choice of "trust" is linked to the intimate relationship recounted in this novel, and the precarious psychological
game that ensues. Interestingly, it is the Latin *confidentia* that
is closer to the English connotations of boldness, audacity, and
impudence. I justify my choice in the end because the first def-
inition of the verb *confido* in my Latin dictionary is, in fact,
"trust." Though come to think of it, I might have called this
novel "Twist" or "Turn" instead.

This is the third of Starnone's novels I have translated in a
span of six years, and it completes a certain cycle. It is not the
final installment of a trilogy, but certainly the third side of a tri-
angle. All three books feature diverse first-person narrators,
tense marriages, fraught relationships between parent and
child. Running themes include a quest for liberty, the collision
of past and present, building a career, fear, aging, anger, medi-
ocrity, talent, and competition. Read in a row, one seems to
emerge from the next. But for those who have read the rest of
Starnone's considerable body of work, this final installment is
in conversation with those that precede it, and for those reading between the lines, there is not only a great deal of intertex-
tuality with other authors but a subtle "intratextuality" with
previous works—Starnone standing in for other Starnones, for
prior Starnones, if you will.

In this novel, a man and a woman—formerly a couple, and
a true marriage of minds, though they never actually marry—
look back and take stock of how the circumstances in their
lives changed. This was also my state of mind as I began translating *Trust* in Princeton, New Jersey, in the spring of 2020.
Until then, I kept hoping that the novel Coronavirus was a
fleeting term, and thus a fleeting problem. I kept assuming that
my son, who had been living and studying in Rome until he
abruptly boarded a plane for JFK the day after Italy went into

national lockdown, would soon enough fly back to finish high school with his classmates. I assumed my husband and daughter and I would fly to Rome, too, to celebrate his graduation. When I realized that none of this was going to happen, I turned to Starnone's Italian instead. I printed out one page each day to make the experience last. The irony of translating this novel just as our day to day lives had significantly changed was not lost on me. And there was another layer of irony I appreciated, one that involves Starnone's impeccably accurate and hilarious description of the vicissitudes of being a writer, and of publishing one book to the next—from composing to editing to reviewing proofs to traveling to sleeping in hotels to speaking in rooms full of people to signing copies to going out to dinner afterward—all of which I recognized, some of which I have had the pleasure of doing in Starnone's company, and much of which neither he nor I could any longer do.

The play of substitution can be distilled into the sentence I love most in this novel, in which an open umbrella, blown by a sudden gust of wind, turns "from a cupola into a cup." It is a stroke of genius. In Italian, "*mutare da cupola in calice*" means literally, to change from a cupola into a chalice. What Starnone evokes here is a change of form, both visually and linguistically. But the wordplay (I'll be so bold to say) is even more satisfying in English, with the progression from cupola to cup. The sentence doesn't end there, however. It continues: "How easy it is to change the shape of things with words" ("*com'è facile cambiare a parole la forma delle cose*"). That *forma* takes us straight back to Ovid, and to the opening words of *The Metamorphoses*: "I*n nova fert animus mutatas dicere formas / corpora*" ("My soul is inclined to speak of forms altered into new bodies"). Ovid's verb *dicere* ("to speak") also echoes Starnone's pithy first line, which poses as a question: "*Amore, che dire?*" ("Love, what to say?"). Starnone may be a builder of rollercoasters, but he is also a master of the backward glance, and his ferocious tales are always tempered by a keening spirit that harks back to Greek and Latin elegy, but also has the universal resonance of popular lyric. Paul McCartney put it this way: "I said something wrong now I long for yesterday." Think of that line when you think back on themes of language and love in this novel.

During the pandemic year that I have spent in the company of this novel, my understanding of *invece* changed just like an umbrella in the wind, from an everyday workhorse in my Italian vocabulary to a lexical distillation of pure poetry and philosophy. From book to book, this type of revelation is what translating my friend's work has taught me about language and about words—that they change as we blink and that they are rich with alternatives. It is my engagement with Starnone's texts over the past six years that has rendered me, definitively, a translator, and this novel activity in my creative life has rendered clear the inherent instability not only of language but of life, which is why, in undertaking the task of choosing English words to take the place of his Italian ones, I am ever thankful and forever changed.

ABOUT THE AUTHOR

Domenico Starnone was born in Naples and lives in Rome. He is the author of fourteen works of fiction, including *First Execution* (Europa, 2009), *Via Gemito*, winner of Italy's most prestigious literary prize, the Strega, *Ties* (Europa, 2017), a *New York Times* Editors' Pick and Notable Book of the Year, and a *Sunday Times* and *Kirkus Reviews* Best Book of the Year, and *Trick* (Europa, 2018), a finalist for the 2018 National Book Award, the 2019 PEN Translation Prize, and winner of the 2020 John Florio Prize.